# TATTOOED LOVE

# TATTOOED LOVE

# BY JIM SNYDER

jms books

Tattooed Love

The following stories were published elsewhere: "Inked in Blood" in the anthology *Perchance to Dream* by J.M. Snyder; "Matching Tats" in the anthology *Vic and Matt Book I: Origins* by J.M. Snyder; "The Tattooed Heart" in the anthology *Hard at Work* by J.M. Snyder.

JMS Books LLC
10286 Staples Mill Rd. #221
Glen Allen, VA 23060
www.jms-books.com

ISBN: 9781468030112

Printed in the United States of America

## Other anthologies by J.M. Snyder

*Ask for them at your favorite GLBT bookstore
or visit jms-books.com*

*For all my tattoo artists who did such wonderful work*
*and inspired these stories.*

# *Fillin' Chet*

CHET SWEARINGEN TURNED off Broad down an unlit side street. This wasn't a part of Richmond he normally visited during the day, let alone at a little after 10:30 on a cold night in February. His car's heater was turned up full blast, the seat warmer keeping his butt and legs cozy, but a scrim of frost clung to his windshield that the wipers and defrost hadn't managed to clear away. It was late and cold and, by the looks of things, he was the only person alive in the world.

*Bad idea*, he told himself over and over again. *Bad idea, bad idea.*

On Tuesday nights he took a lecture class at Virginia Commonwealth University downtown. It ended at ten, and he usually headed straight home. But when he checked his cell phone during the break, he found a cryptic text message that sent tingles of anticipation from his head to his toes. *All clear. Want 2 hook up?*

He hadn't been able to type the answer fast enough. *YES!*

The rest of the class had passed in a blur. Afterward, he hadn't lingered with the other students, instead making a beeline for the parking lot. The frost on his windshield hadn't deterred him; he just cranked the heat up high and set the wipers on full speed, shivering as the late model Lexus he drove warmed in the frigid night air. When a small patch of clear window finally appeared, he hunkered down over the steering wheel to see through to the road and inched out of the parking lot. Thank God it was late—his was practically the only car on Broad.

Off campus, he kept up the snail's pace because he wasn't familiar with the area. Anything Southside was beyond his ken—he lived in a loft apartment in Richmond's fashionable West End, and the rundown section known as Churchill wasn't a place he liked to go. Lord knew he heard about it often enough in the news, shootings and robberies were commonplace in that part of the city. Even though he saw no one on the streets, he felt them watching him, assessing him. Young preppy college kid, in a fancy car, heading...where?

Even he didn't know. He felt like a mouse crawling across a room full of cats. The felines would only feign disinterest until they knew they had him trapped.

He shook his mind to clear that image away. At the corner, he turned right and let his car pull into the center of the narrow street. Vehicles lined both sides of the road, closing in on him. The houses he passed were dark, but he saw glints of life on the porches, his headlights catching a bottle of liquor here, a spoon for freebasing there, white eyes in hidden faces watching him pass.

*Bad idea.*

Another block, two, and he spotted a familiar street sign. Despite the fact he was the only one on the road, he turned on his signal and took a left. Suddenly the residential homes were behind him, and a row of dingy storefronts stared blindly as he passed. He was looking for one in particular...

*There.* On the corner sat a squat building whose neon lights were dark, though through the front windows Chet could see a faint light deep within, like a flame flickering against the night. He passed the side street, hit the brakes, and with one arm thrown over the back of the passenger seat, he steered as he backed the car into the turn. He could've just pulled in and parked, he knew, but he didn't like parking on the wrong side of the street, even if he *could* get away with it. That wasn't the way he'd been taught.

The car's tires kissed the curb and he corrected his aim, straightening out. The moment he cut off the engine, cold air seeped into the car. *You can do this,* he told himself, taking a deep breath to calm his nerves. *You're already here.*

That made him think of Scott. Fumbling his cell from his coat pocket, Chet called up the last message received and hit REPLY. *Just parked. Meet me at the back door.*

He toyed with the idea of something more—*love you* came to mind—but it was still early in their relationship, and Scott didn't seem the type to toss around words like that, anyway. If Scott ignored it, Chet would be hurt, no matter how much he tried *not* to be. Better to leave things the way they were between them. For now.

Message sent, he shoved the cell back into his coat pocket and pulled the keys from the ignition. When he opened the car door, a whoosh of icy air curled around his legs. As he stepped out, a puddle limned with thin ice crackled underfoot. Slamming the door shut behind him, Chet crammed his hands into his pockets to keep them warm.

Across the street, he saw three shadows detach themselves from the darkness and head his way.

*Shit.* He huddled into his coat and skirted the front of his car, gaze trained on the building's employee entrance a few yards away. Behind him, he heard shoes scuffle over gravel, and a reedy voice called out, "Yo, man. Hold up. You got any change?"

Chet ignored the plea and picked up his pace.

"Fucker!" another man spat. "Hey, I'm talking to you!"

A third voice chimed in. "Look at them wheels, man. He *got* to be loaded."

"I'ma ask you again," the first man hollered. "Then I'ma

gonna take your money anyway."

His friends laughed. They sounded closer now, but the door was only a few feet away, if that. Chet didn't want to break into a run, but he stepped faster, clutching his cell phone deep in his pocket as if for protection. *Bad idea, bad idea!*

A short set of stairs led up to the entrance. Chet tried to take them two at a time but slipped on a sheath of ice and had to clutch at the icy steel railing to keep from falling. More laughter, right up on him now, so damn *close*. His heart hammered as he lunged for the door. The knob was like the railing, almost too cold to hold. He gave it a hard turn—

It was locked.

*Now* he looked back at the three rough guys following him. Dressed in a ragtag assortment of clothing, they wore woolen caps pulled down over their ears and temples, and unkempt beards obscured most of their features. One held a bottle of alcohol hidden in a paper bag; another had a hand-rolled cigarette sticking out of the corner of his mouth. When the wind shifted, Chet caught the bitter whiff of marijuana and grimaced. Where the hell was Scott?

"Hey, man," the lead guy said, his voice low now, almost intimate. "How much you got on you, bro?"

Before Chet could gather up the courage to speak, the door behind him scraped open. Heated air rushed around him like an embrace. He turned and found himself face to face with Scott.

*Thank you*, Chet prayed, knees weakening at the sight of the strength curled in those wiry arms.

Tall and lean, Scott looked incredibly sexy in his wifebeater tank top despite the cold, arms covered with ropy muscles hidden beneath full sleeve tattoos. A pair of ink-stained jeans hung low on his hips, and buzzed blond hair gave him a military bearing. He had piercings up both ears, in both eyebrows, and in both nostrils.

Scott barely spared Chet a glance, instead glaring behind him at the trio of degenerates. "Chino!" he cried, recognition coloring his voice. "You fucking ass! What the hell are you guys up to, scaring my man like that?"

The leader of the group—Chino—raised both hands in surrender. His friends backed away, already losing interest. "Scotty, dude, sorry. I didn't know you two were friends. I was just looking for some change."

Scott laughed, a loud, booming sound that seemed odd coming from someone so damn skinny. "Roll him and it's no more free ink for you, motherfucker. I got his back."

Chino nodded quickly. "Sure, man, whatever you say. Hey, you got anything you can spare me for?"

Standing aside, Scott nodded behind him into the building as if to tell Chet to get inside. He didn't need any further prompting—Chet brushed past Scott gratefully and rubbed his hands together to warm himself up. Scott rummaged into the front pocket of his jeans, the motion tugging them dangerously low. Chet found himself staring at the twisting ivy vines tattooed into the small of Scott's back, just above his tailbone. *Hurry, please.*

Pulling out a rumpled dollar bill, Scott stepped out onto the stoop to hand it over. "Don't fuck with his car, either," he warned. Chet saw him hold onto the dollar even as Chino grabbed it, unwilling to let go until his words elicited a nod from the other guy. "Now go on, get out of here. The ABC over on Pink is probably still open this late. You and the boys warm yourselves up with a little Jim Beam."

Chet shivered as Scott lingered outside. Watching the guys walk away, probably, making sure they didn't plan to circle back and vandalize Chet's car. After a long moment, he came in and shut the door behind him, pushing against it to make sure it locked.

Suddenly alone with Scott, Chet let out a breath he hadn't known he'd been holding in. "Jesus," he said, rubbing his arms to bring the warmth back to them. "Who are they?"

"Just some bums who hang around here," Scott said with a wave of his hand. "It's a tough neighborhood—"

"No shit," Chet muttered.

"I give them free tats to lay off my customers. They aren't bad kids. Just bored." If Scott was bothered by the cold, he didn't show it. Closing the distance between them, he held out a hand for Chet's coat. "Let me hang that up for you."

Reluctantly Chet unzipped his coat. When he pulled one arm free, Scott took the empty sleeve, so Chet pirouetted to slip the other arm out, as well. He smoothed his sweater down over his flat stomach, frowning at the hint of an erection already bulging below his belt.

He felt a hand brush his cheek, then Scott's fingers rubbed under his chin to grip it. Chet's breath caught in his throat as he found himself forcibly turned to face Scott.

Pale hazel eyes glared at him, almost golden in the overhead lights. For a long moment they stared at each other, Chet's gaze shifting from Scott's left eye to his right eye and back, Scott unnerving in his intensity. "What?" Chet finally whispered.

Scott's fingers pinched either side of Chet's jaw as he pulled Chet close, closer, until their lips pressed together with a demanding kiss. An eager tongue barged its way into Chet's mouth, claiming him. Scott released his grip on Chet's chin and let his hand trail down the front of Chet's sweater, over Chet's belly, to rest on the belt cinching the jeans around Chet's waist. Two fingers dipped under the sweater then behind the belt, tickling tender skin.

The kiss relaxed, deepened, as Scott's initial lust mellowed. Chet gave into him, melting beneath Scott's touch. Against Chet's mouth, Scott whispered, "Ain't nobody gonna fuck you but me."

Chet went limp at the promise. Maybe this wasn't such a bad idea after all.

SCOTT HARRIS WAS the kind of guy Chet had always wanted and never thought he'd actually have. That might have explained his interest in dating the tattoo artist, but what Scott saw in him, Chet didn't know.

Growing up, he'd always been the good son—academically minded, he did well in school and got a full scholarship to the state college of his choice. A nerd, some might have said, if it weren't for the fact he played football and basketball as well as studied hard. Well-rounded, then, with a promising future ahead of him. His father anticipated one day hiring Chet into the fold of the family banking business, like his older brother before him.

But at college, he majored in art history instead of business, a choice that didn't sit well with the folks. His mother liked to use the excuse he was a *double* major to explain why, at twenty-six, he hadn't graduated yet. She failed to name those majors unless prodded for the information. She didn't like his second choice of journalism any more than the first.

Chet himself said he was on the long-term course plan, on his way to becoming a professional student. The problem was, his parents had his future already laid out for him, and the only way he could think of to avoid it was to draw out the years he stayed in school. So after a full credit load his first semester, he dropped down to part-time status and moved off-campus. He got a couple of jobs to help pay rent—one at Richmond's art museum, another in the editorial office of a weekly local newspaper that catered to the college crowd. The dangling carrot his father held out—a forty-plus hour work week wearing suits and ties, managing portfolios and mergers—didn't entice Chet. When he turned twenty, his mother had said he was simply sowing his oats. Six years later, she no longer laughed at her own little joke.

He met Scott in the art museum, of all places. The guy was a tattoo artist who rented a booth at a dive in the seedier part of the city—not anywhere Chet would normally be caught *dead* at. Even with his bohemian spirit, he still had standards. The Lexus he drove was a gift from his father; the clothes he wore came from Abercrombie and Fitch. He knew some people might've pegged him as a hipster, and he even looked it up once online to see what it meant, but he didn't like to label who he was, no matter how *hipster* that thought might be. As long as he didn't turn out to be his father, Chet didn't care what people called him.

When the museum where he worked hosted an exhibit on local tattoo artwork, he checked it out on his lunch break, not so much because he liked tattoos, but because his father did not. Personally, Chet thought they hurt, and he wasn't sure he wanted to commit something to his skin he'd be stuck with for the rest of his life. But guys with tattoos were pretty damn hot, and Richmond was ranked as the third most tattooed city in the nation. Sometimes it seemed *everybody* had a tattoo except for him.

The exhibit stayed busy, and the lunchtime crowd pressed against the large prints of tattoo designs by local artists didn't appear to be in any hurry to move aside. Chet had a half hour—he spent fifteen minutes jostling aside people so he could catch a glimpse of a few of the prints. What he saw didn't really impress him. Some Celtic designs, a full back mural inked to resemble the ceiling of the Sistine Chapel, shoulders and arms covered in images copied from photographs. Finally Chet pushed his way to the exit, shrugging his polo shirt back into place. With any luck, the museum's cafe wouldn't be quite so crowded, and he could still grab a bite to eat before he had to get back to work. Something on a pita, perhaps, with hummus on the side.

As he waited in the serving line, he glanced at the hand holding the tray next to his. Black ink swirled around the back of the hand, and letters spelled out something on each knuckle of the fingers. What Chet had thought at first glance was the colorful sleeve of a shirt turned out to be more tattoos. He let his gaze trace the designs—over the wrist, around the forearm, coalescing around the elbow, then higher, over the bicep. Every inch covered in ink. How long would it take to explore it? To follow the patterns with his finger or—God, he didn't dare think it, did he? With his tongue. Did the skin taste differently? What would it look like against his own unblemished flesh?

He felt a thrill run through him and flushed. None of the guys he'd ever messed around with had more than a little ink—a cross on the bicep, a rainbow on the ankle, something like that. Nothing this vibrant or blatant. What would his mother say?

The line moved forward but the guy beside him stayed. Chet glanced up and saw piercings, amber-hazel eyes, cheekbones that could cut glass. A studded nose, perfectly heart-shaped lips enhanced by studs above and below them. This guy was *nothing* like anyone Chet had ever met before, but despite that—or maybe because of it—he knew he couldn't let this moment pass away. Clearing his throat, he flashed a smile he knew was dazzling and said, "I like your tattoos."

Those lips pulled into an easy grin. "Thanks, man. You got any ink?"

"Not yet," Chet hedged, shaking his head. "I've been thinking about it, though."

*Yeah, like for two seconds,* he added silently, but if it kept them talking, the little white lie would be worth it.

It was. Scott introduced himself and told Chet he'd done a few of the tattoos on display upstairs. They chatted as they stood in the serving line, and after Scott had checked out, he stood to one side, tray in hand, obviously waiting for Chet. Without being asked, Chet followed him into the dining area, the two of them snagging a seat by a window that looked out over the busy downtown traffic. Conversation sparkled between them, Scott obviously very animated when it came to his art. By the time he was finished with his sandwich, Chet realized he was falling for the heavily inked guy. Scott even had him half-convinced he needed to get inked.

Too soon, Chet realized he had to be back at work. He stood and, holding his tray, tried to think of what to say to make Scott want to see him again. The problem was, Chet didn't know if Scott was sending off all the right signals or if he just got turned on talking about tattoos. Was it him? Or the thought of reeling in a potential new customer?

"Here." Scott dug a business card from his back pocket and handed it to Chet. "I rent a booth there. Hit me up sometime."

Chet fingered the card. "I'm not sure I'm ready to go under the needle just yet…"

Scott shrugged, then gave Chet such a steady stare, it unnerved him. "I'm not talking about just *that*. Unless you want me to spell it out—"

"No, I got it," Chet said with a relieved laugh. He pocketed the card and held out his hand for Scott to shake. "Looking for a good time, call."

"Definitely." Scott set his elbow on the table, arm up as if preparing to wrestle. He gripped Chet's hand like that and, instead of shaking it, gave it a gentle squeeze that belied his rough appearance. One finger slipped between their clasped hands to tickle Chet's palm. "Call me."

"I will," Chet promised. His whole body tingled at the thought. "Definitely."

CHET TOOK THE plunge and called Scott a few days after they met, and they went to a midnight movie playing at the Byrd in Carytown. They sat in the back of the theater where no one could see them and, at some point, Chet stopped paying attention to the film and began to realize Scott's hand rested high on his leg. He covered it with his own, pulling it toward him. Scott took the invitation and reached across the armrest to cup the crotch of Chet's khakis.

At the touch, his cock went from mild arousal to full-blown hard-on. He stared at the screen ahead, no longer comprehending the images flickering across it, and held his breath as Scott slowly unzipped his pants. *Yes,* he prayed, *yes, yes.* Fingers fumbled into his open fly, digging into his underwear, to encircle his stiffening erection.

*Yes.*

Then he was out in Scott's palm, the cool air of the darkened theater and the thrill of excitement at what they were doing fanning the flames of lust igniting his veins. He gasped as Scott began to massage his dick, and let himself slide down into the seat a little, his legs spreading farther apart. How things had managed to move so fast between them, Chet didn't know, but he didn't dare question it. This was exactly what he'd hoped to get from the evening.

The movie played on. At some point, Scott leaned over into Chet's lap and kissed the weeping tip of his cock. The tattoo artist then opened wide and took Chet's length into his mouth. Chet felt a ball piercing in the middle of Scott's tongue as it tickled down the slit in his dick. With one knuckle between his teeth to keep quiet, Chet thrust up into Scott, losing himself in the sensations, the emotions, the moment, the man. Later, when Scott kissed him goodnight, Chet swore he could still taste himself on Scott's lips.

And that had just been the beginning.

Chet kept odd hours—he went to school during the week, held down the museum job between classes, and spent his weekends copyediting for the newspaper. Scott ran his booth at Tattoo 804 six days a week from noon to eight, taking a break on Thursdays when he got paid. Things moved fast between them— less than a week after they met, they were having sex in the back seat of Chet's Lexus. It was much roomier than Scott's VW Beetle, to be sure. He wasn't quite ready to invite the guy back to his apartment yet, and maybe that was part of the reason why Scott never brought Chet back to the place he called home.

They didn't need to, Chet reasoned. The car worked well down darkened side streets or in abandoned parking lots. A few times, he'd snuck Scott into the employee restroom at the museum for a quick fix, and there was a supply room in the back of the tattoo parlor that locked from the inside. Whenever one of them wanted to get off, he texted the other. *Want 2 hook up?*

Every time Chet saw the text on his cell phone, his cock

began to swell.

He didn't want more, he told himself. He didn't *need* more. Scott didn't seem interested in taking things further, and Chet was sure as hell not going to be the one to suggest it.

THREE MONTHS LATER, Chet still wouldn't necessarily call what they did *dating*. If he had to put a name to it, he'd call them fuck buddies. Though he had to admit, if only to himself, that he felt something more for Scott. After all, he let the guy talk him into getting a tattoo.

He felt rebellious doing it, more nervous than scared, and almost chickened out twice as he flipped through the racks of flash designs looking for the right one. Finally he told Scott, "Nothing really stands out to me. You decide."

"Where do you want it?" Scott asked.

It was late evening—Chet had stopped by after class but the tattoo parlor was still open for another hour, so if he wanted to get off, he had to wait for Scott first. As much as Chet would've loved to get a tattoo somewhere obvious, like the crook of his elbow or the inside of his wrist, he didn't have enough courage to so blatantly disobey his parents. "Maybe on my back," he suggested. "Like partway down the middle where no one can see it unless I show them? What do you think? Will that hurt?"

"Shit," Scott drawled with a laugh. "It's going to hurt no matter where you put it."

Chet winced. "How much?"

"Don't worry—I'll be gentle." Scott gave him a seductive wink that sent shivers down Chet's spine. "We'll take it in stages, how's that sound? Just do the outline tonight, and get you back in here for the fill later."

The parlor was mostly empty, but Chet still stepped closer to Scott and lowered his voice to tease, "I thought I was here to get *filled* in the first place. If *somebody* would just get off already…"

Scott grinned. "What? You don't want me to wait for you?"

NOW IT WAS four weeks after Chet's first tattoo. True to his word, Scott only inked in an outline of the image—what would eventually be a complicated half-moon/half-sun orb hovering just behind him was currently a series of black lines indicating the design. It'd hurt like a bitch, and Chet dreaded filling it in. Couldn't they leave well enough alone? True, it looked silly as is—Chet caught sight of it in the mirror sometimes when he was getting into the shower and shuddered to remember the way it'd felt, as if someone were scraping into sunburnt skin. When it was finished, it would look bad-ass, Scott promised...and he'd never lied to Chet before. In the meantime, it just looked bad.

As Chet followed Scott through the employee-only area of the tattoo parlor, he wondered what had the artist working so late. Part of him was afraid to ask. What if he wasn't Scott first booty call of the night? What if he wasn't the main course but dessert? What if—

"We threw a birthday party for Lanie after work," Scott said, interrupting Chet's thoughts. "I knew it'd run late, but geez. They closed the place up early and it was beers all around. I thought they'd never leave."

Lanie was one of the piercers at Tattoo 804. When Scott first introduced them, she told Chet she'd love to see him with a Prince Albert. He'd laughed politely at the time, but when he went home and Googled the term, he almost fainted. No way in *hell* was he ever getting one of *those*! And if he did...God forbid, but if he *did*, she'd never see it.

"Did you give each other tattoos, too?" Chet asked as Scott held the door to the main area of the tattoo parlor open for him.

The look Scott threw his way reminded Chet just how little he knew about the art. "You don't ink someone who's been drinking."

Chet shrugged; he didn't know. "I guess you guys don't need alcohol to dull the pain."

He followed Scott across the darkened floor to his 'booth,' a stool, a padded tattooist chair stretched flat into a tabletop, and a series of locking steel drawers that held all his ink and supplies. Only a few of the recessed overhead lights were on— the bulk of light came from a small lamp perched on a desk beside the chair in Scott's booth.

"It thins the blood," Scott explained. "If you've been drinking, then you bleed more when you get a tattoo. And it hurts a hell of a lot worse than usual."

"But you're too drunk, you won't feel it as much," Chet muttered under his breath.

If Scott heard him, he chose to ignore him. Instead he stopped in mid-step, so abruptly Chet bumped into his back. Turning, Scott was suddenly *right there*, right in front of Chet, so close he just had to pucker his lips to claim a kiss. His hands roamed the front of Chet's sweater, finding the hardened nubs of Chet's teats beneath the fuzz and plucking them erect. He trailed down Chet's stomach, over ticklish skin, to play with the snap fly of his jeans. *Snap*, open. *Snap*, shut. Open, shut, open, shut, a steady rhythm that punctuated their kiss. With each snap, the zipper beneath it eased down a little farther than before. Chet wondered how many kisses it'd take to get him out of the jeans altogether.

Apparently Scott had other plans. Slipping his hands under Chet's sweater, he rubbed up the flat plane of Chet's belly and around his waist. "Let's see how well you've healed," he whispered against Chet's lips.

For a few seconds longer, Chet lost himself in their kiss and didn't let his mind register Scott's request. *How well I've healed...* What did that mean, exactly?

Then it hit him. *My tattoo.*

Taking a step back, he let Scott pull his sweater up as he turned. In the full-length mirror on the wall across the room, he could see his reflection in the mirror beside Scott's booth, but the tattoo itself was hidden by Scott's body. Chet savored the artist's sexy image—the way his jeans rode low on his hips, how his top pulled taut to tuck into his jeans, the colorful tattoos up and down his arms and across his back…Chet could faintly see them through the wifebeater. *Mine*, he let himself believe, if only for the moment.

Scott ran his hand over Chet's back, then tugged the sweater up higher. "Take this off."

Chet obeyed, slipping the sweater over his head. When he held it to his chest, his arms still in the sleeves, Scott grabbed both his hips and positioned him to get a better look at the tattoo. His touch was ticklish, smoothing down Chet's spine. Chet winced in reflex at the memory of pain. He didn't really need anything else done to the image. No one would know the difference but him.

"Looks real good," Scott murmured. Chet watched in the mirror as Scott leaned over to kiss the black lines on his back. Then he asked the one question Chet dreaded. "Ready to fill it in?"

Chet tried to step away but Scott's hands on his hips held him in place. "I thought you wanted to have sex."

"We can do both." Scott stood and, looking over Chet's shoulder, met Chet's gaze in the mirror. "All my supplies are here, *you're* here, and no one else is around. Who's to say we can't get a little…"

He ground his hips into Chet's buttocks. A hardness strained at the front of his jeans, exciting Chet as it rubbed against his ass. "You mean do it here?"

Scott gave him a sardonic grin. "The tattoo, shyeah. The sex, why not?"

*Why not indeed?* Chet knew there had to be a million reasons why not, but with Scott's erection pressed tight against his butt, he couldn't think of a single one. Still, his voice quivered when he said, "Sure, I guess."

"Lose this." Scott tugged on the sleeve of Chet's sweater as he headed for his booth. "You ever done it on one of these? They're designed for comfort."

"I've never even *been* in one before I met you," Chet reminded him. He shrugged off the sweater and folded it, then set it on a stool in the booth beside Scott's. His hands strayed to his belt, still buckled even though Scott had unsnapped his jeans. Over his shoulder, he asked, "These too?"

Scott was rummaging in one of the drawers, pulling out tiny bottles of ink and placing them on a steel tray nearby. He glanced up and winked, sending a spark of lust shooting through Chet. "Unless you want me to fuck you *through* them..."

Quickly Chet unbuckled the belt and unzipped the jeans. He shoved them to his knees, then kicked off both his sneakers and the jeans at the same time. Bending in just his briefs, he shook the wrinkles from the jeans and folded them, too, setting them on top of the sweater. The sneakers he lined up and nudged under the stool.

A cold, slimy hand touched the inside of his inner thigh. Chet squealed and whirled to find Scott snickering, his hand wet with clear A&D ointment. "What the *hell*!" he cried.

Scott laughed. "You're fun to tease. Come here." When Chet didn't move immediately, his tone hardened. "Come here."

The floor felt as cold beneath his socked feet as the gel did, smearing between his thighs. He closed the distance between them, wary. He loved being with Scott—the mere fact that a guy like *that* could ever possibly be interested in a guy like *him* still amazed him sometimes. He loved the way Scott looked, every inch of him, piercings and tattoos included. He loved Scott's light eyes, like windows full of unblemished sunlight shining from his rugged face. He loved Scott's laugh, his smoked-out voice, his rough kisses and strong hands, and the way their bodies fit together so perfectly during sex. Shit, if he were being honest, he would admit he loved *Scott*, period, but he wasn't quite ready to go there yet.

But Scott had a bad streak in him, too. The tattoos and

piercings hinted at it, and Chet knew that streak was part of the reason he was falling so hard for the guy in the first place. Sex with Scott could be a little harsh—never violent, but Scott liked to bite and pinch and thrust hard. He normally wanted to be on top, but a few times when he'd let Chet take control, he'd wanted more. The last time, Chet had to squeeze the base of Scott's balls in a tight fist and hold it there as they fucked; Scott wouldn't let him let go until Chet climaxed. Only then could Chet relax his grip, allowing Scott's orgasm to erupt from an almost purplish blood-filled cock. He liked tweaked nipples and love bites in tender places, like the inside of Chet's thighs, and he'd even mentioned felching once, though the look on Chet's face had stemmed that conversation real quick. Chet didn't even know what it was at the time—he had to look it up, too, and wondered if the librarians at the university ever wondered which student was Googling odd sex terms on the school computers—but it didn't sound nice. It wasn't.

Now Chet almost feared Scott. The cold hand on his leg had been one thing; would it be twisted titties next? Snapped waistbands or a bitten lip? Sometimes Chet wondered what had ever made him think he could control a man like this in the first place.

The ink and tattoo machine sitting out on the tray beside Scott's stool didn't go unnoticed. Chet hoped they fucked first. Maybe then he could talk his way out of any more artwork. He'd like a full-blown, gorgeous tattoo—who wouldn't? But he was a bit of a wimp when it came to pain.

When Chet was close enough, Scott reached out and grabbed the front of his briefs to reel him in the rest of the way. The slick hand ran down Chet's flat, pale belly. "You're so virginal. No piercings, no ink," Scott murmured, tugging Chet's briefs down to expose the hardening dick hidden within. "And then there's this."

Chet's cock swung up to meet Scott, the tip drooping slightly from its weight. Scott trailed the cool ointment down the path of tiny hairs leading from Chet's navel into his pubes, then grasped Chet's dick at the base. Tucking the briefs below Chet's balls, he palmed the fuzzy nuts and leaned forward, mouth open wide, tongue licked out. Chet watched Scott's mouth zero in on him, his breath caught in his throat as that pierced tongue came closer, and closer...

With a gasp, he closed his eyes as Scott swallowed his cock. The warm, familiar mouth worked his length, the ball piercing bumping along veined skin as Scott sucked. The hand around his shaft kneaded him, the other hand rubbed his balls. He felt like he was being milked, every nerve in his body attuned to the sensations in his crotch, every synapse gearing up toward release. Chet ran his hands over the scruffy top of Scott's short-cropped hair, tugged on the hoops ringing his ears, fucked into him, eager for this, *this*, here, now, *him*.

Before he could come, though, Scott pulled free. Chet's spit-slicked dick hardened in the cool air, and his balls shrank when Scott's warmth was gone. Only half-kidding, he said, "That was cruel."

"That was just the warm-up," Scott replied. He slapped Chet's ass, leaving a greasy palm print on his briefs. "Take these off and we'll get to the main event."

Chet pushed down his briefs, but stopped at mid-thigh when Scott reached out to caress his legs. "This good?"

Scott stood, his hand trailing up Chet's body and around his waist to pull him into a one-armed embrace. "Perfect," he murmured, catching Chet's mouth with his.

The kiss was gentle, a stark contrast to the press of Scott's body against Chet's. Chet felt himself pinned between the tattooist chair and his lover, both unyielding as they hemmed him in. Without releasing Chet's body—or lips—Scott half-turned and unzipped his jeans. The low-riding pants slipped to his knees, followed by a pair of boxers hastily unsnapped. Then Chet felt Scott's erection alongside his own, both cocks gripped together in one tight fist. His lover's hardness surprised him; how Scott had managed to stay seated with *that* crammed down the front of his jeans, Chet didn't know.

For a long moment, Chet concentrated on their kiss, the tender tongue inside his mouth, the metallic taste of the piercing at its center, the way the ball rubbed the roof of Chet's mouth. Scott stroked their shafts with long, languid movements, fingers squeezing as he traced up and down the lengths, the saliva on Chet's dick adding lubrication to Scott's. With his hands on the tattooist chair behind him, Chet held his own against Scott, wanting everything the man could offer, eager to prove he could take it.

Then Scott's lips kissed across Chet's jaw to his ear. "Bend over," he purred.

The words warmed Chet up inside and tickled deep within him. *Yes.*

Scott stepped back just enough to let Chet turn in place. He fondled his cock as he watched Chet assume the position— hands flat on the padded surface before him, legs stretched as far as the briefs trapping his thighs would allow. He glanced to one side and could barely see them in the mirror on the far wall—the angle was bad. But to his right, if he leaned forward a little, Chet could see enough in the other mirror to fuel his desire. His ass in the air, waiting. Scott jerking his dick as he stared at Chet's backside, ready to dive in. *Yes.*

As he watched in the mirror, a feeling of detachment descended over him. He saw Scott squat behind him, saw Scott's hands reaching for his ass cheeks a second before they touched his buttocks, lifted them, separating him so Scott had complete access to his innermost spot. He saw Scott lean forward, tongue darting out, then felt that hot, wet organ lick his anus, rimming him. "God," he gasped, clenching the chair beneath him, as Scott's tongue squirreled inside him and that damned piercing rubbed over super-sensitive skin, breaching his hole. His cock throbbed for release, his balls ached. Though he didn't mean to, he stood on tip-toe as lust washed over him. "Please, please, *please.*"

Scott's tongue fucked him, in and out, its piercing triggering a furious storm of sensation flooding Chet. Damp fingers worked him wider, slipping inside, making way for the main event. Chet pressed the side of his face flat against the leather chair and watched in the mirror as Scott fingered him with one hand. With the other, he raised a condom packet to his mouth and tore it open with his teeth before expertly rolling it onto his own cock. Chet watched him guide the thick, veined member closer.

A moment later, he felt the flared tip butt between his ass cheeks.

With a grunt, Scott thrust his hips and shoved his cock inside.

Chet moaned with pleasure. The leather had warmed beneath him, slightly damp from condensation and a little drool. "Yes," he sighed, arching his back to raise his ass to his lover. Scott found a hard, steady rhythm, one Chet was familiar with, and their bodies bumped together at a furious pace. Chet closed his eyes, giving into the fucking, savoring the fullness in his ass for as long as it would last. He didn't have to see Scott's hands on his hips in the mirror—he felt them there, holding him in position as Scott pistoned into Chet's ass. Eventually one would find its way beneath Chet to jerk him off as Scott came. It would be fast. Sex between them usually was.

So when Scott screwed himself in as far as he could go and stopped, Chet opened one eye, curious. He felt as if he stood on the edge of a precipice of desire that yawned before him, the other side just out of reach. One push, maybe two, and he'd take the plunge. He'd fall headlong into ecstasy. He'd come in a rush of delight that would leave them both breathless.

Then why had Scott stopped?

The answer came in the form of a dull drone behind him. He recognized that sound, all too well. Pushing himself up off the chair, he glanced over his shoulder and saw Scott fiddling with the frequency on his tattoo machine, the needles buzzing in one hand.

Chet's gaze swept the table beside Scott. Ink poured into tiny containers, ready to use. A&D ointment dolloped into a gelatinous blob to one side. The latex gloves on Scott's hands—when had he put those on? The napkins to wipe away ink and blood, the disposable razor to shave the area, the antibacterial soap to clean the wound…

"Whoa," he cried. He clenched the muscles in his ass around Scott's cock to get his lover's attention. "What the hell's all this shit?"

"Relax," Scott purred.

Chet didn't see how he could. "Aren't we in the middle of something here?"

The smile Scott gave him looked slippery. With a wink, he set the tattoo machine down, the buzzing ceasing. But he picked up a napkin and the razor, and placed his hands on Chet's back. Firm. There was no arguing with the strength in those hands. "I've always wanted to do this," he said as he drew the razor gently down Chet's back. "The endorphins are going to drive you crazy—"

"You're doing a good job of that yourself," Chet muttered. He tried to squirm but couldn't get out from under Scott's hands. "Can't we just wait until we're done fucking before you get into…this?"

The soap was next. Scott squirted it onto Chet's recently healed tattoo, the liquid cold as it ran down his lower back and over the curve of his ass. A few drops found their way between his buttocks to sting his widened hole. "Scott, please."

Scott kissed Chet's shoulder and stayed there, hunched over him, until Chet turned to look back. His leonine eyes were so beguiling, Chet felt any fight go out of him. "Trust me," Scott whispered, his breath hot against Chet's skin.

Chet couldn't believe it, but he did.

With a wiggle of his hips, Scott reminded Chet just how intimate this moment was between them. Chet felt his libido surge as the cock in his ass bumped his prostate, and between his legs, his own erection throbbed. Scott shoved in as far as he could, shifted his weight from one foot to the other to settle in, then leaned down over Chet's back, one hand holding the skin taut beneath it, the other poised with the tattoo machine humming in his grip. "Hold absolutely still," he breathed.

Chet went rigid with nervous anticipation. This was going to hurt, he knew it. It'd been a bitch last time and he'd told himself he'd never let Scott talk him into any more ink…

Then the needle touched his skin and Chet didn't dare breathe. It didn't feel quite as bad as he remembered. Sure, it stung a bit, but it felt like a burn he might get from having sex on a low, scratchy carpet. Maybe it was the needle itself—Scott had told him the last time that the fill work would go easier than the outlines. Maybe it was the fact this wasn't his first time under the gun. Maybe he'd blown the first experience up too much in his mind and nothing could've been as bad as he remembered.

Or hell, maybe it was the hot guy plowing him from behind as he got inked, he didn't know. But other than the constant droning in his ears and an itchy feeling on his back, the tug of Scott's hand as he manipulated Chet's skin, the press of Scott's wrist against Chet's spine as he plied his art, Chet didn't really feel it this time.

Carefully, he rested his chin on the leather table before him. "That doesn't feel too bad," he admitted.

"It's the endorphins kicking in," Scott said. He raised the tattoo machine off Chet's skin and jiggled his hips a little, sending sparks of electric lust flickering through Chet's groin. "Your body's in overload at the moment. Sex and pain are just two sides of the same coin."

Chet didn't answer. Instead, he placed his face on his hands and watched his body in the mirror, watching Scott peer over his back, hard at work. Every so often, he'd pause and move around a bit, reviving the sexual energy between them. When he had to lean back to get more ink in the needle, he'd thrust in and out of Chet's ass a few times, just to keep them both aroused. Time passed in a carnal blur, the sensual drawn out to extremes. Part of Chet ached for immediate release, an end to this exquisite torture, but part of him hoped the night would never end.

After a while, Scott turned off the tattoo machine. Silence pressed in around them. He set the needles aside and shook his hand, fingers flexing to work the life back into them. "Enough playing around," he growled as he gripped Chet's hips. "You ready to come?"

"Oh yeah," Chet moaned. Was he ever.

His back stung from the fresh ink, but when Scott began to fuck him in earnest, the feeling dissolved between the ardent waves of rapture roiling through him. Scott eased a hand beneath Chet, catching his rock-hard cock in a fierce grip and pumping it as they moved together. The added friction pulled Chet on toward orgasm. Hugging the tabletop, the leather heating beneath his quick breath, Chet gasped, "Yes," and "God," and "Scott, please, God, *Scott!*" as his lover rode him into the chair. When he finally came, his cock shuddered as ropy jism spurted into Scott's palm.

A few seconds later, he felt Scott's release fill him inside, the hot surge igniting another, more powerful climax within Chet. He came again, knees weak, legs shaking, arms locked tight around the tattooist chair to keep him from puddling to the floor in a satiated heap.

*God.* Yes, Chet was sure of it now. This was love.

THE TATTOO WAS completed fully clothed. Or rather, Scott was clothed—Chet pulled up his briefs and put his jeans back on, but left his sweater folded on the stool. Lying on the tattooist chair, he stretched out with his arms folded under his head and watched his lover work in the mirror. Scott seemed intent on his art, his hands sure and strong on Chet's back. Chet kept quiet, wincing only once or twice when the needle stung a little. He was afraid to speak, really. Afraid that if he did, he'd say something he'd regret.

Something like *I love you*.

He did, he *knew* he did, but he also knew saying it out loud might scare Scott away. He didn't want to chance it; he'd rather savor the few stolen moments they had together than risk them for the hope of something more. So he held his tongue and watched Scott, his heart swelling, his throat full with emotion he didn't dare admit.

Scott moved to Chet's other side, his back now to the mirror. Chet could no longer see his hands, so he shifted his gaze to Scott's face instead. No longer a reflection in a mirror but here, right over his shoulder, brows furrowed in concentration. The tip of his tongue peeked from between his lips. Chet remembered the feel of that warm muscle on his dick, in his mouth, in his ass. *Love you*, he thought, projecting the words as if Scott would somehow hear them in the buzzing of the tattoo machine between them.

With a sigh, Scott turned off the machine and wiped the ink and blood off Chet's back. "There. Done."

"How's it look?" Chet asked. He sat up a little and tried to look at the design, but couldn't see it.

"Awesome, of course." Scott set the machine aside and grabbed the bottle of liquid soap, squirting a stinging spray onto the tattoo as he wiped it clean. "The first of many, I bet."

Chet wasn't so sure, but he knew better than to say anything. He struggled to sit up. "Let me see."

Before Chet could slide off the chair, Scott barred his way, grabbing his arm in a fierce grip until Chet met his stare. He knew what was coming before Scott leaned in to claim an insistent kiss. But what Scott murmured into him took his breath away. "Come home with me tonight."

"What?" Chet pulled back in surprise.

Scott didn't drop his steady gaze. "You heard me. You can say no."

"I'm not saying no." Chet's mind reeled—this was something new for them, the next step, a turning point in their relationship.

To be honest, he didn't know *what* to say. Did Scott know what he was asking? Did he even suspect what it meant to Chet?

Scott's hand tightened on his arm. "You're not exactly saying yes, either."

"I'm just…" Chet shrugged, at a loss for words. Finally he admitted, "I don't know what to say, really. We've never…"

"We could." Scott relaxed his grip and rubbed his hand down Chet's arm. The touch was soft and comforting. "I like you, Chet. I know I haven't exactly put it into words but I'm not the type to go around saying shit I don't mean. Tonight—it was special. You can't deny it."

Chet assured him, "I'm not."

"It meant a lot to me," Scott continued. He dropped his gaze to his hand, now trailing over Chet's forearm. "*You* mean a lot. I want you to know that. I want…"

Chet held his breath, afraid any move he made might make this moment disappear. "What?" he whispered. "What do you want, Scott?"

Scott's hand folded into Chet's, and he raised his eyes to meet Chet's. "You. Only you."

Something burst deep within Chet, flooding him with a warmth that tingled down his spine. He threw his arms around Scott in a tight hug. He felt kisses on his cheek as Scott carefully hugged him back, arms around Chet's waist to avoid hurting his new tattoo. Into Scott's ear, he sighed one word.

"*Yes.*"

# *Inked in Blood*

I DECIDED TO get my last tattoo on a whim. It was late in the evening, almost nine o'clock, but the red *Open* sign still blazed outside Tattoo 804. I could see the neon as I cruised down Broad Street, heading home from what had turned out to be a wasted night. The guy I'd been seeing on and off the past few weeks had chosen tonight to break things off with me…*after* I paid for dinner, of course. So I wasn't in the best of moods as I shifted gears, trying not to hit any of the lights as they flickered from green to red along Richmond's main drag. I missed the one just before the tattoo parlor, and my brakes squealed as I ground to a halt at the intersection a block away. As I revved my engine, I stole a glance at Tattoo 804's large, inviting windows—the pool table inside called my name, and I could think of a place or two on my body that needed new ink. Before I could change my mind, I stepped on the gas pedal and shot through the light when it finally turned green, coasted across two lanes of traffic, and eased to a stop at the curb in front of the place.

By the time I got inside, though, I began having second thoughts. It *was* getting late, and I didn't want to do anything I'd regret in the morning. I didn't see any hours posted on the door, but I also didn't see anyone else, either. I was the only customer in the whole place, and I couldn't hear anything over the pounding hard rock music that pulsed from the walls to tell me I wasn't alone. No buzzing needles, no employees chatting it up in a corner, nothing. Raising my voice, I called out, "Hello?"

I was just about to say fuck it and leave when a guy ducked through a pair of swinging doors that led to a back room. He was my age, late twenties I'd say, of average build, wearing a pair of baggy shorts and an oversized tee under an open button-down shirt that made me peg him as a skater type. A battered cap worn backwards on top of his head hid a head full of peroxide colored curls, but his sideburns and goatee were natural, dark. An earring pierced one bushy eyebrow; another pierced the middle of his nose. His mouth didn't smile when he looked at me, but his eyes did—large, chocolate eyes, expressive, soft. Despite the tattoos up and down his forearms, despite the rings in his brow and nose and lip, I could stare into eyes like that and lose myself, easily.

Despite the night I'd had, my body trilled with lust when those eyes met mine.

"'S up, man?" he asked with a slight nod my way.

Suddenly self-conscious, I pointed behind me at the door for no real reason and asked, "You guys closed?"

He sort of shrugged. "What do you want?"

That didn't really answer my question. But he didn't exactly turn me away, so I moved closer to the counter between us and tried to tear my gaze from his. I couldn't. "Just a small tattoo. Right here." I pointed at a spot on the left side of my chest, above my heart. "I don't know what. Just some sort of cool tribal design, I guess. Or hey, how about a nice dotted line with the words, *Insert knife and twist?*"

With a laugh that didn't quite earn me a smile, he asked,

"One of those nights, eh?"

"I've had better."

Leaning on the counter, he appraised me for a long moment, silent. I was just about to ask if maybe he wanted to lock up the place and hop in my car for a spin, see if he couldn't improve my mood, when he reached down to flick a switch just out of my sight. Behind me, the *Open* sign winked out. "Latch the door for me, will you?" he asked. "You're my last customer of the night. We'll see what we can come up with."

"Naw, man," I said, shaking my head. "If you have to get home…"

*Now* he smiled, finally, and it'd been worth the wait. White teeth flashed at me, even and strong. The front ones were slightly large and he had a faint overbite that was more than a little cute. In fact, for a moment he seemed to be nothing *but* teeth, flat incisors, sharp cuspids, slightly round premolars, a mouthful of perfect dentistry leering at me. His eyes flashed with a hungry gleam that made my cock swell in my pants.

I wondered if my evening wasn't starting to turn around.

WHEN THE GUY told me his name, I heard "Chris," but I had to sign a waiver and he'd written *Rist* as the tattooist on the form. I said it softly under my breath, "Rist," and figured it was probably the most off-the-wall nickname for Christopher he could come up with that wasn't already commonplace. As I handed back the waiver, I said, "Cool name."

He shrugged and looked over my driver's license. "I like it. You go by Tommy, Tom, what?"

I wished I had a neat derivative to call myself, but I didn't. "Tom's fine. Tommy. Whatever."

If I had hoped for a second smile, I didn't get it. Instead, he nodded at the panels of preprinted tattoo art that hung beside the counter on poster frames. "Why don't you pick out a design while I set things up? Won't be long."

"What kind of price are we looking at?" I asked.

Rist held up his hand, forefinger and thumb about an inch and a half apart. "Stay within this size and I'll say for you…sixty bucks. It'll take about an hour."

"Cool."

Shoving my hands into the pockets of my jeans, I began browsing through the art panels and hoped something would stand out. It was hard to concentrate—all I could think of was the pressure in my pants, my thumb pushed tight against my dick, and the bite of my underwear in my balls. From the corner of my eye I watched Rist write up the necessary paperwork. Whenever he glanced my way, I hurried to look busy, flipping through the artwork in search of something, *anything,* to get inked onto my skin. This wouldn't be my first tattoo—I had my initials on the back of my arm, just above my elbow, and my college mascot on my right shoulder. So yeah, this wouldn't be my first lifelong regret. But on the front of my chest, I'd see it more often, in the mirror staring back at me or when I looked down at my naked body, so I needed something I'd at least like after tonight. Something neat, something me.

Most of the preprinted tattoo art consisted of pin-up girls. Half-naked chicks cavorting in seductive poses weren't exactly what I wanted on my body—how would I explain a buxom brunette to the next guy I fucked? I wasn't bi, wasn't even in-terested in the fairer sex. The panels that weren't nude girls were demons, skeletons, or the like. It was sex or death, all geared toward the straight man. I wanted to ask where the happy queer section might be, but I suspected there wasn't one.

"Find something?"

Rist's voice startled me. He stood so close behind me, I could feel his breath on the nape of my neck and the warmth of his chest against my arm where mere inches separated us. When I moved back, his hand touched my waist for a brief second before falling away. Suddenly my mind was blank, my cock raging in my pants, my blood surging in my veins, and my mouth unable to work. "Um…"

This close his eyes were mesmerizing. His gaze dropped to a spot on my neck and a hint of a smile flickered across his lips, showing me those pointy cuspids again. "See anything you like?"

Would *you* be the wrong response?

When I didn't answer right away, Rist leaned past me and flipped to the next panel. The sexy she-devil was replaced by a giant crucifix; he flipped again, quickly, never taking his eyes off me. The next panel was covered with scrolls and hearts. "How about someone's name, maybe? Your lover?"

"God, no." I shook my head for emphasis. "I'm doing this to forget about him. The dick."

Rist moved closer—I felt his chest against my back, a barely there touch I wanted to step into, but I didn't dare. Though we were alone in the tattoo parlor, I was well aware of the bright lights overhead and the full-length windows facing out onto Broad Street. Anyone driving by could glance in and see us easily. Two men looking through tattoo designs, standing a little too close to leave much else to the imagination. The breath on my neck was soft and ticklish, and when I shifted from one foot to the other, I felt something hard and uncompromising against my ass for a brief second before Rist moved back.

So I wasn't the only one turned on by this. In my pocket, my hand pressed my dick flush against my body and I had to bite my lower lip to stifle the moan that wanted to escape.

"How about one of these?" Rist purred in my ear.

He had stopped on a panel of dark images—jagged gravestones like crooked teeth, bats rose below full moons, black cats arched and hissing. Twin holes mimicking fang bites dripping with blood. Vultures in cemetery trees, and ghosts holding decaying banners on which were written sayings like *Death Before Dishonor* and *Only the Good Die Young*.

I turned the panel before Rist could. "I want something a little more real," I told him.

With a breathy chuckle, he asked, "You don't think this stuff is real?"

He was pointing at the next set of tattoos, which showed cartoonish horror monsters like werewolves and vampires. I threw a sardonic look over my shoulder and found him close enough to kiss. I could see the exact spot where the peroxide stopped just above his ear and the dark brown of his natural hair color took over. What were we talking about again? "Please."

From the corner of his eye, he glanced at me. Then he smirked and ducked his head, resting his chin on my shoulder a second before stepping back. "They're out there, man," he said, moving away and ruining the moment. He lifted the panels and started looking through them quickly, searching for something. "The books and movies have it all wrong, though. They aren't scary creatures, you know? Aren't out to kill everybody and shit. They don't *sparkle*, for Christ's sake."

I laughed. "Do they even drink blood?"

His hands froze in mid-flip and he looked back at me, eyes wide. "Oh, yeah. They drink blood, all right. That part's dead on."

So the guy was cute with a monster fetish. He worked in a tattoo parlor—it didn't surprise me he liked strange things. I rocked back on my heels and glanced around, wondering if it was too late to call the whole thing off. I mean sure, it was nice of him to stay late and agree to give me a tat. But it'd been a spur of the moment decision and given the night I'd had, I couldn't be blamed for calling it off now. Sleep on it, come back in the morning, see if I still wanted to go through with the ink. Chances were the answer would be no. Would Rist really get all that upset if I changed my mind?

Before I could ask, he found the panel he'd been looking for and flipped to it. Standing aside, he asked, "What about any of these?"

My resolve crumbled when I saw the page of rainbow flags, pink triangles, and lambda designs. One in particular caught my attention, a small pride flag that looked as if it had been painted on with jagged strokes of a small brush. "That one," I said, pointing it out. "That's it. That's what I want."

Rist gave me that semi-smile of his that lit up his eyes more than his lips. "Cool. I'll set up my station and we'll be good to go."

"How'd you know?" I asked. When his gaze dropped to the front of my pants, I pushed down my erection and hoped he didn't think the hand in my pocket was doing just that. "I'm usually a pretty good judge with guys but you're hard to read. When I first came in here, I would've sworn you were straight."

His smile cranked up a notch. "Sometimes, but not tonight."

That sounded like a promise.

HIS STATION WAS near the back of the tattoo parlor, out of sight from anyone passing by on the street. Not that there was much traffic at this hour. This late in the year, the sun went down a little after seven and by now it was almost ten, dark out beyond Tattoo 804's windows. Here and there street lamps cast small cones of yellow light on the sidewalk, and the traffic stop in front of the parlor flickered from red to green and back again as if winking into the night. But anyone still out was downtown at the clubs, or just driving this stretch of road heading home. I wondered why Rist didn't just throw me out with the rest of the garbage. He had to have someplace to go for the night, something better to do.

As I stared out the window at my car parked at the curb, I watched the reflection behind me in the glass and waited to see Rist motion me over. I wouldn't be able to hear him over the music blaring through the speakers—he hadn't bothered to turn it down, and every so often I'd swear it cranked up another notch, if that was possible. Why it needed to be so damn loud, I didn't know. I felt like I was in one of those clubs down on the Slip...all I needed was a drink in my hand, a few hard bodies grinding against mine, and I'd be good to go.

A hand fell to my shoulder and startled me. "You ready?"

I jumped to find Rist beside me. "Jesus," I swore, my heart stuttering in my chest. His sudden nearness did little to alleviate the throbbing in my dick. "I didn't see you come up, man." So much for watching out for him in the window.

With a nod, he indicated I should follow him back to his station. A black tattooist's chair had been set up facing the wall. Next to it was a moveable arm rest and a tall stool where Rist would sit. By the stool was a tray on wheels, the kind dentists use, where wrapped packages of needles and bottles of ink were already set out. "Shirt off."

I glanced around at his station as I obeyed. Lurid posters from B-grade movies covered the walls, screaming odd titles like *Plan 9 from Outer Space* and *Amazon Women from the Avocado Jungle of Death*. Rist seemed to have a thing for monsters—action figures of Dracula, Frankenstein, and the Wolfman were lined up along a table behind his stool or leered from wire baskets hanging from the wall, where his inks were stored. A plastic cabinet of drawers was covered in stickers for bands I had never heard of before, with names like Satan's Death Candy and Screaming Monkey Stick. I shrugged off my shirt, tossed it to the floor, and did a slow pirouette to try and see everything at once. Strange place, Rist's corner of the shop. Then again, I probably would've been disappointed if it wasn't a little freaky.

He fiddled with the tattoo guns and glanced over at me, hands on my hips, eyes wide as I took it all in. Again his gaze dropped to my waist, and this time I didn't have a shirt to pull down over my erection. With a nod at the chair, he told me, "Sit. I can re-do the ink on your arm if you want."

I had to climb up into the chair, using foot rests a good twelve inches off the ground. As I settled in, I took a critical look at my college tattoo and grimaced. The once bright blue had faded to a sickly hue, the yellow almost the same tone as my skin. Once it had been my school's logo, a golden lion's head mascot circled with my college colors and the name of the school underneath. Now, if I squinted right, I could just make it out. But it was a fairly large design—much bigger than the inch and a half Rist had shown me earlier—and I wasn't up for spending more on tonight's adventure. "What'll that cost?"

Rist dropped onto the stool and wheeled up beside my chair. He fiddled with a control somewhere out of sight and I dropped down a little, until we were eye-level. For a moment he set his elbow on the arm rest as his fingers played across the skin on my shoulder, feeling the outline of the tattoo. His touch was cool, sending a shiver down my spine that jolted my already stiff dick. I shifted in the chair uncomfortably, pulling at the front of my jeans just a little, hoping I played it off without him noticing. This close, how could he not?

Then his hand trailed down, fingertips like ice as they played over the hairs on my forearm. Goosebumps rose in his wake. I watched his movements, slow, deliberate, my gaze glued to his tattooed hand. At my wrist, he rubbed a tender spot just above my thumb and I turned my hand over, laying it open for his. When I looked up, I found him staring at my face with something akin to desire. My voice croaked when I tried to speak and I had to clear my throat to be heard over the music. "How much?"

"Tommy." The way he said my name sounded like a purr, low and soft. I didn't hear it so much as feel it echo through me, the same way I felt the beat of the music reverberate through my spine. "We're both adults here. *Alone.* I'm sure we can come to some kind of *mutual* agreement."

Still thinking money, I started, "I don't want to spend too much…"

His hand closed over mine, his palm cool against my heated fingers. With a gentle squeeze he released me and moved lower—down my leg, along my thigh now, angling toward my crotch. A second before his fingers brushed over my sheathed cock, I realized what he was suggesting. He confirmed it when he said, "I was sort of thinking something else."

For a long moment, I was too stunned to speak. My dick throbbed in his grip, eager to take him up on his offer. I'd been propositioned before—hell, many times, and probably would be again before the week was out. But I hadn't seen this one coming. Could I possibly get a free tattoo out of it?

Shit, for a blowjob, or something more? I'd fucked guys for less.

Rist must have thought I was unsure because he tugged on my zipper a little, pressing it into my dick as he did so. "Come on, man," he cajoled. "Either you're hard for me or you've got some sort of medical condition that gives you elephant balls. This place is dead. So we can take care of each other and you get a tattoo for your trouble, what do you say?"

I laughed. "What do *you* get from it?"

His smile turned enigmatic. "I get off. What more can I ask for? I'm a little…"

He said something then that I didn't quite catch. *Horny*, I thought, but the music seemed to swell and drown him out, or maybe he just dropped his voice a little. I watched the shape his lips made around those pointed teeth of his and what might have been *horny* could just as easily have been *hungry*, as well. Either way, the message was clear. He wanted me as much as I wanted him.

I'd be a fool to turn him down.

Bringing my hand up, I covered his where it rested on my crotch. At his slight grin, I dipped my fingers under his and plucked the zipper from him. I eased it down and almost sighed with relief as my dick protruded through the open fly, released at last. The tight prison of my jeans disappeared, swelling my already erect cock. Rist rubbed my length through my underwear, tracing the outline of my dick from thick base to damp tip. I leaned back in the tattooist's chair and let my hands fall to the sides, gripping the plastic leather as I bit my lower lip in ecstasy. A guttural sound escaped my throat, something primal and raw, that rumbled through my body like the music. "Yes."

With his fingers kneading my dick, Rist leaned down and

stuck out his tongue to lick along the tattoo on my arm. From the edge of my vision I watched—he trailed around the outline with the tip of his tongue, his breath feathery and light, his touch wet, maddening. He licked his way around my bicep, into the spot where my arm and body met, and up my clavicle to the hollow of my throat. The wisps of bleached curls peeking from under his cap tickled my chin. I arched my back slightly to get a better look at him only to find him staring back, pinked tongue stuck between perfectly white teeth that seemed to have lengthened since the last time I noticed. Maybe the movie posters and action figures surrounding us had something to do with it, but this close to my neck, his teeth looked wicked.

Free tattoo or not, suddenly I wasn't too sure. "Hey," I whispered, the word lost in the music.

Rist closed the distance between us, moving so quickly I didn't have time to turn away. He pressed his mouth to mine in a fierce kiss that left me breathless, his tongue delving between my lips with a possessiveness that piqued my already sore cock, causing it to jerk in his hand. For someone with such a slight build, he was quite powerful—he held me back to the chair with the weight of his kiss alone, the fingers at my groin rubbing into my underwear. As our kiss deepened, he got up under my dick and guided it out, pulling down the underwear until the elastic waistband bit below my balls. The cool, air conditioned air hit my heated member and pricked it harder. Rist laid it flat against my body, tip pointing toward my navel, and drew concentric circles in the sensitive skin between my dick and balls as I whimpered beneath him.

Lust roiled through me. I grasped at the seat beneath me, then at his shirt to pull him closer, then his pants because I wanted them gone. "Please," I murmured into him. My tongue glanced over his sharp teeth and danced away, preferring the smooth surface on the front of his incisors or the impossibly soft places on the inside of his cheeks. My hips bucked off the seat, rubbing my cock against his arm as he toyed with me.

"Rist, please. Yes. Fuck, yes."

Pulling back slightly, he kissed the corner of my mouth and asked, "You have a condom?"

*Shit.* I better. If I didn't, we were cutting off a finger from one of his disposable latex gloves and using *that*, I didn't care. I needed in him, now. As I reached for my wallet in the back pocket of my jeans, Rist stood and wiped his mouth with the back of his hand. His lips were swollen, red, *too* red, almost bloody, but I ran my tongue over my teeth and couldn't feel any cuts on it. Hell, I couldn't feel much of anything, to be honest—his kisses had left me numb. My whole mouth tingled like it did after I had gone to the dentist to fill a cavity and the Novocain started to wear off. Then I licked my lip and tasted a strange spot on it. A small wound, as if I had accidentally bitten myself while eating. "Did you bite me?"

When I raised a hand to touch it, Rist was there in my face again. "You're fine," he said, kissing the corner of my mouth again—the spot I had found. "Are we good with the rubber or do I have to run down the street to the 7-11?"

Since my lip didn't hurt, I ignored it and concentrated on more pressing matters, like praying the condom I usually keep tucked in the back of my wallet hadn't fallen out or otherwise disappeared since the last time I checked. It hadn't—it was still there, the package wrinkled but unopened, hidden inside a carefully folded twenty I kept on hand for emergencies. I held it up and started to say something witty, but whatever that might have been dried when I saw Rist shrug off his shirt.

Silver hoops pierced both nipples. A dark cloud covered his torso, tiny black spots that swept up from the waistband of his pants to billow out across his abdomen into a cloud of bats. They looked almost real, bursting from him in search of food. As they rose up his chest, they grew larger, more distinct; I saw eyes and sharp teeth cut out of the shapes, and each wing ended in a long claw. The cloud rose before him, washing his pale skin with color, before tapering to one large bat at the head of the pack. It flew directly under Rist's left nipple as if aiming for the ring above it.

As he shucked off his pants, the bats seemed to burst from the black curls at his crotch. With each move he made, the cloud seemed to flutter and flex against his skin as if in flight. He turned as he stepped out of the pants and I saw an articulated spine tattooed down his back. Leathery wings graced his shoulder blades, more demon than angel. They arched across his back, each extending out onto his arm before ending in claws similar to those on the bats' wings. My gaze dropped to his round ass, where the spine tattoo disappeared between his fleshy buttocks. On his left cheek was a tattooed bite mark, two deep puncture wounds dripping with blood, as if some sex-crazed vampire mistakenly sank his fangs into Rist's ass instead of his neck.

He kicked the pants aside and turned toward me again. I asked, "Let me guess—vampire bats?"

With a grin, he ran his hand down his chest in what appeared to be a familiar gesture, starting from the first bat down through the cloud, until his fingers delved into his pubes. An erect cock jutted toward me, the skin ruddy and veined. It arched up at the end, just enough to show me the piercing underneath the tip. "You fuck with that thing in?" I asked, pointing.

When he thumbed over the ring, my stomach gave a queasy little flip. "You wouldn't feel it through the rubber. Bareback, though…I'm told it tickles."

My stomach clenched at the thought of being pierced *there*, but my balls throbbed at his near nakedness and when he brushed his hand across the top of my thigh, my cock jerked toward him. "My condom, my call. Sit up on me already, will you? Let's get going. You've got skin to ink."

The look in his eyes excited me. He leaned in close and for a moment I thought he was going to steal another kiss, but at the last minute he dropped into my lap, his mouth closing around the tip of my dick. I couldn't feel those sharp teeth of his now—he had his lips tucked over them, and that soft tongue licked down my length like it was candy. He took me completely in, bobbing between my legs until I felt the sideburns on either side of his head tickle my thighs. I leaned back, raised my legs a little, and thrust into his hot, willing mouth. "Yes!"

He came up, lips massaging my shaft, letting me slip free. When he reached my tender cockhead, he paused to kiss it, almost sucking, as he tongued the slit splitting the spongy tip. I gripped the sides of the chair and bucked into him, wanting more, needing release. "Fuck," I muttered, watching him watch me, my dick caught between his lips. A slight pressure pulsed at the base of my glans, as if he were very gently *chewing* on me. I felt a spurt of pre-cum and struggled to rein in my desire. "Please, God."

My juice bubbled from his lips as he let me go. With one last lick, he took the condom from my limp hand and tore into the wrapper with teeth that glistened wetly in the overhead light. "God's not here at the moment," he purred, unrolling the rubber down my shaft. "Tonight you're all mine."

Reaching over beside my chair, he pulled his tray of supplies closer. Before I could ask what he was doing, he grabbed a jar of A&D ointment, unscrewed the cap, and scooped out a handful of clear lubricant. He coated the condom with it, working down and around the length of my cock, then motioned for me to come closer. I wasn't sure what he meant, but when I held out my hands he smeared first one, then the other, with the goo. Setting the jar back on the tray, he nudged my foot aside where it sat on the foot rest. "Let me step up."

My feet spread, allowing him to stand on the chair. It lurched beneath his sudden weight, then sank back into position when he climbed into my lap. With his knees on either side of my thighs he knelt before me, dick swaying in my face. I leaned forward, tongue outreached, and found the cold metal piercing underneath his dick. Just thinking about it made me shiver, but my tongue toyed with it, curling to stick into the ring, then flattening the metal against Rist's skin.

"Fuck me," he growled.

I needed no further prompting, but he took both my hands in his and guided them to his ass as he thrust into my mouth. My fingers eased into the crack between his buttocks and I spread the slick lubricant down hidden skin, seeking entry. When I found it, my forefinger wriggled inside, turning in a widening circle as I loosened him. His cock butted against my lips and he gripped the chair behind my head as he rocked back into my hands. His breath came in harsh gasps above me. When I finally managed to catch his jittery dick in my mouth, he sighed and pushed his length fully into me as he pounded the chair with one fist. "Yes! Yes!"

The chair squealed dangerously beneath us. I pulled him toward me, closing the distance that separated us, until his legs were splayed as far as they could go and I had to stoop down to keep sucking his cock. Blindly I grasped my own hard dick and held it with one hand as I spread him wide with the other. His dick slid from between my lips with a wet sound lost amid the music and moans. Trailing saliva-slicked kisses up his abdomen, over the cloud of bats, I traced his navel with my tongue and told him, "Sit."

As he did, I guided myself into him. My fingers squeezed the head of my cock as I worked it into his tight anus, while the fingers on my other hand held him wide. Inch by inch I eased inside, past the first band of constricting muscle, my dick beating in time with the music and my heart. He caught my face in both hands and raised it toward his, mouth covering mine as he slowly sank down onto my hard cock. I thrust up, my hands under his buttocks as I pulled him close, his dick between us bumping my navel and leaving a trail of damp jizum behind. "Yes," he moaned into me, sucking on my bottom lip. When he leaned back a little and looked into my eyes, I felt that stare deep in the pit of my stomach, and his lips were once again red and wet. His words were nothing but sighs, full of longing and desire, full of want. For me. "Tommy, yes. *Yes!* Uh uh uh."

Each time he made that sound, he rocked above me and my cock shuddered within his tight ass. His weight ground my balls into my thighs as he moved his hips against my groin. When he leaned back, I supported him with both hands, thinking he wanted a different angle. His sphincter clenched around my cock, working me toward release. With his body exposed to me, I nipped at one nipple playfully, then kissed my way down his chest one bat at a time. Faint drops of red left bloody imprints behind. He'd bitten me again.

Then he placed a hand on my shoulder to stop me. I sat back against the chair, my hips making tiny little thrusts as I fucked into him. With hooded eyes he grinned at me, his tongue licking his upper lip as if drinking away the taste I had left behind. "About where do you want that tat?" he asked.

I ignored him and closed my eyes, giving into the sensations—the heat of his body around my dick, the weight of him in my lap. I don't chat during sex. Another few minutes and we could pick up where we'd left off with the ink…*after* I came.

Rist had other plans. He pinched my nipple to get my attention, twisting the tender bud. The pain shot from my chest straight to my rigid dick and I gasped his name. "Here?" he asked, pointing above my left breast. "This a good spot for you?"

"Yeah, sure," I sighed. I picked up the pace, really thrusting into him as hard as I could. He rose in my lap like a boat on rough waves. "Wherever. Just let me…"

*Finish*, I wanted to say, but I didn't get the chance. With an impossible strength, he clamped his knees against my thighs, stilling me. I froze in mid-thrust, my dick held prisoner in the clenched muscles of his ass. I glanced at his enigmatic grin and wondered why we had stopped. "What?"

"Here?" he asked again, pointing to a spot just over my left nipple.

Confused, I nodded a little. Catching his dick in my hand, I massaged his length as if to entice him to get back where we had been two seconds ago. My thumb rubbed up the underside of his shaft, toying with his piercing each time I bumped against it. "Yeah, that's good. I thought we were sort of in the middle of something here. Can't this wait? I'm almost done."

Rubbing my sore tit, he squeezed his knees into my thighs. With an arched look, he laughed. "No, we're not. We're just getting started."

I didn't know what he meant by that—myself, I was so close to coming, I could feel my balls drawing up in anticipation of shooting my load. But once again I was surprised by his strength. He made it impossible for me to move my hips up, down, or sideways. His legs and ass had me pinned in place. I felt like a drop of water beading on the end of a leaky faucet, filling with fluid, waiting for the moment when I could fall. "Please," I sighed, tugging on his dick. "I need this."

"We'll get there," he assured me. Then he leaned behind him and snagged his tray of tattoo supplies. As it rolled closer, I watched him reach for the jar of lube again. Maybe my hands were a little dry and he wanted to slather them so I could jerk him off as I came. Sounded good to me.

But instead of the A&D ointment, he picked up the tattoo gun instead. With a flick of his thumb, the machine buzzed to life in his hands. I felt its vibrations through his body and down my dick as the entire chair shook beneath us. I tried to keep my voice even, but it trembled slightly when I asked, "What are you doing?"

He ground his hips into me, jolting my stiff cock. "Inking you. That's why you're here, right?"

I watched him reach for a small spritz bottle of green surgical soap. "You're kidding. *Now?*"

He squirted the bottle, dispensing cool spray against my heated skin. "Hold still," he said.

Was he *serious?*

IN DISBELIEF I watched him prep the spot where my tattoo

would go. He wiped away the soap with an unused Burger King napkin, then leaned back to pluck a disposable razor off his tray. Each move he made shifted his position on my cock, pulling it this way and that, bringing a wave of new sensations crashing over me. Deftly he shaved the area above my tit, then wiped it with the napkin again. The raw, red skin looked new in the overhead lights.

And he was impaled upon my dick the whole damn time. If it weren't for the pulse of his body throbbing around my member, I would never have believed we were still joined together. Instead of wilting, my erection seemed to swell within him, building with unspent energy, waiting for release. I dug my fingers into his meaty buttocks and massaged his ass, hoping he'd take the hint—put down the tattoo gun and fuck me, already! When he didn't, I growled his name. "Rist."

"Quiet." A dollop of gel soothed the razor burn, then he placed a template of the tattoo onto my chest. Carefully he peeled it away, leaving the image drawn on me. He sat back to inspect his work, rocking back on my dick. My eyes slipped shut as I hissed in delight. "There. That look good to you?"

Without opening my eyes, I murmured, "Hmm, yeah." I thrust into him a little and felt the ring on his dick bump into my navel. "Fuck me, Rist. Forget the tattoo for a moment, will you? I'm about to bust a nut."

His eyes sparkled wickedly. Grasping my arms, he wriggled his hips into my crotch as if he were trying to screw himself down tight onto my dick. I picked up the pace, bucking beneath him, hurrying to get off. Just as I felt myself at the brink of orgasm a second time, he stopped again. My mind reeled, thick with lust. "What the hell…"

The tattoo gun started up in response. Nerves churned in my stomach as I watched Rist dip the needles into a small pot of purple paint. "You're not really going to," I started. Then, when he positioned himself in front of me, one hand pulling the skin on my chest taut while the other drew the tattoo gun closer, I gripped his knees and tried a different approach. "You know this can't be sanitary."

A smile split through the concentration on his face. "You're so far inside my ass, I can taste you in the back of my throat," he said softly. "How sanitary is *that?*"

"It was your suggestion," I countered.

"You didn't say no."

Before I could think of a reply, the needles touched my skin. Heat erupted from the spot but there wasn't any real pain. It felt like a mean carpet burn, nothing more. Still, between the buzz of the machine and the pinpricks of discomfort, I turned my face and flinched, even as my dick quivered with need. But I wasn't about to move and mess up the artwork, no matter how close I might be to release. I held my breath and waited until he paused, reaching for a napkin to wipe at the excess ink, before I allowed myself a short, quick thrust into him. "Please," I sighed.

He didn't answer.

I looked at him and saw raw hunger light up his eyes as he stared at his handiwork. His whole face seemed to glow with desire. I glanced at the beginnings of the tattoo, but there was nothing out of the ordinary about it. Beads of bright blood bubbled up through the ink—as I watched, one burst and trickled down my skin, over my nipple, before Rist's finger flicked out to stop it. In a hushed voice, he murmured, "Hot damn. You're a free bleeder."

"Sorry?" I asked, unsure what he wanted me to say. "Is that going to be a problem or something?"

"Or something." He raised his finger to his face as if he were going to sniff my blood on its tip, or maybe do something incredibly kinky like draw it onto his cheek like war paint. I bit my lower lip, waiting. If he did that, *Jesus.* How fucking sick is *that?* I'd probably come as he did it.

But what he did instead shocked me more, literally. I never considered myself overly kinky, but I felt a jolt of electricity shoot through me, invigorating my senses. Like a lightning bolt, it ripped down my spine and into my erection, and I couldn't hold back any longer. As his finger disappeared between his lips, his tongue darting out to taste my blood, my dick erupted in him with an explosive rush.

"*That's* sick," I said with a shaky laugh.

He grinned. "You liked it. Got you off, didn't it?"

I couldn't deny that. "What's it taste like?" I wanted to know, fascinated.

"Blood," he said, shrugging. "Warm, living, succulent. A little sweet, if I'm being honest. You taste good."

A flush burned my face. "Yeah, and you know that how? Who else's blood have you had lately?"

His lips parted in a smile that displayed those sharp teeth of his. His tongue licked over them, ruddy with my blood. In his face I saw more than I wanted to know. The pieces began to fall into place—his strength, his speed, his fetish with monsters. No, not monsters, not exactly.

With vampires. What had he said to me? *They're out there, man.*
Shit.

I forced a laugh that sounded anything but funny. "You're kidding me."

His gaze never left my face. I watched, fascinated, as he leaned toward me, his rigid dick prodding against my belly the closer he got. I thought he planned to kiss me, let me savor the coppery taste in his mouth, and my chin jutted out, lips pursed, waiting. My cock began to stiffen again at the thought.

At the last moment, he dipped his head, the curls of his bangs tickling my face. I leaned back, giving him my neck. Isn't that what vampires wanted? The jugular? I moved my hips beneath his, stirring my wilting erection back to life.

But no—he moved lower still, tongue out to trace the curve of my neck. He planted a kiss in the dimple above my clavicle, then another right above where he'd begun the tattoo. Through hooded eyes I watched, my breath short, staccato bursts that caught in the back of my throat. He wouldn't…

He did.

With the next lap, his tongue licked over the open wound. I saw the tip turn a deep purple shot through with red swirls of blood. Watching me, he turned up his tongue and rubbed it over his front teeth. The ink and blood discolored them. The next lick wiped them clean.

"Is that safe?" I whispered, my voice barely heard over the music.

"The ink's non-toxic," Rist said, dipping down for another taste. His cock shuddered between us, as if my flesh and blood were orgasm-inducing ambrosia. His lower body moved slightly, grinding into me, renewing my libido.

"I meant...*ahhh*." My words dissolved in a guttural, lusty growl as the muscles in his ass flexed around my cock. I thrust up into him, quick little bursts of energy designed to get me off again. "Yes, yes, *please*, God. That feels good."

With one last taste of my tattooed skin, he wiped the remainder of ink away with a damp napkin. "This won't kill you," he promised. "In fact, you'll probably heal faster, and hey, it's better than taking a bite out of your neck to bleed you dry. Am I right?"

I couldn't form a coherent answer. My head lolled back against the chair, my body trembling with need. When the tattoo gun began to buzz again, I barely flinched. My heart thudded in my chest, my blood surging through my veins to pound in my dick, deep in Rist's ass. Each time he paused to dab away excess ink, I grabbed the chance to fuck him once, twice, three times in rapid succession as he leaned down to lick clean my wound. At some point, he plucked my hand off his waist and guided it to his weeping cock. I thumbed over his swollen tip, toyed with his piercing, tugged him toward release.

The tattoo seemed to take hours to complete. Every nerve in my body felt on edge, every synapse firing, every inch of me raw and bleeding before Rist. An eternity after he had begun, he set aside the tattoo gun and wrapped his arms around me as he pressed his mouth to my new ink. The heat of the tattoo disappeared in sharp pinpricks of pain, and like a child to a mother's breast he sucked my blood through the wound.

I held him to me, my arms over his shoulders to hug him close. His head was cradled between my elbows, and my hands had a tight grip on his ass. I held his buttocks up and apart as I gave into the moment, fucking into him steadily now, the pressure in my dick building as we moved together. I felt sharp teeth scrape over my flesh, short nails dig into my back, Rist's cock pinned fast between us. *Yes*, my mind crowed as I gasped nonsensical sounds on the verge of language. *Yes*, and *please*, and *oh, holy fuck, yes yes yesyesYES!*

My second load burst from me, more violent than the first. A sudden wetness slicked my stomach as Rist came in unison. Sitting up slightly, he raised his head to kiss me, *finally*, to kiss *me*. Blood and saliva trickled on my chest, up my throat, onto my chin. Then his lips covered mine, staking their claim.

TO TOUCH UP the tattoo on my arm, Rist moved to the stool beside my chair. I winced as he worked, but I couldn't deny how turned on I was sitting there naked in the empty tattoo parlor, being inked by the sexy, nude man at my side. Or should I say vampire? I thought it a lot of bullshit, to be honest, but every time he paused in his work, he would lean in to lick away the excess ink and whatever blood rose from the wound. The sight of my bright blood on his lips and tongue excited me all over again, and I sat with cock in hand as I watched him work. Before long I was hard again, my dick aching, my hand fast around the base as my fingers kneaded the veined shaft. My palm pressed into my balls as I thrust into my hand.

"Careful," Rist warned when I moved too much. He would pull the needle away to avoid ruining his work and wait for me to stroke myself a time or two before he grabbed my arm again. His grip was fierce, his hand steady as he worked. From the thin hair at his crotch, his dick jutted out at me blindly. Whenever he licked my tat, his balls drew up toward his groin as if sucked in and his cock jiggled happily. In those moments, when he fed, I jerked my hand up and down my length as fast as I could, hurrying toward release.

As he finished up the tattoo, he wrapped it lightly with plastic wrap he taped into place. Watching the ink and blood splay out beneath the thin covering, I asked, "So now what?"

With a shrug, he told me, "No charge, man. We're good."

I wasn't talking about the cost of the tattoo. "No, I mean...what happens next?"

Rist rummaged around on his tray until he found some papers hidden beneath a stack of napkins. He handed me a sheet, on which were written instructions for caring for the tattoo. "Keep it covered for an hour or so, then wash it real good with antibacterial soap. Don't let anything press up against it while it heals—"

"No, not that." I folded the paper into a small square as I shook my head. "If you're really...*you* know...doesn't that mean I'll turn into one, too? Isn't that the way this works?"

Rist's forehead wrinkled in confusion. "I didn't bite you."

Unconsciously, my hand rose to touch my lip.

He laughed. "That was there already, man. I just picked off the scab. And the tattoos don't count. The needles pierced your skin, not me. I don't go around turning people for the hell of it. Shit, I'm not getting stuck with someone for the rest of eternity, man. That's worse than marriage."

I grinned. I hadn't been aware how nervous I'd been until I felt the knot in my stomach loosen a little. Just to clarify, I asked, "So I'm not going to turn into a bat or anything, right? I won't be burned up when I go out in the sun?"

"Not if you wear sunscreen," Rist teased. "Keep those tattoos out of it, though. You don't want them to fade."

I let out a sigh of relief. "Just as long as I'm not going to start, you know, hunting down young men to suck their blood."

Rist winked at me. "Whatever turns you on. But if you just

want someone sucking on *you*, I'm here any time after six."

A shiver of delight ran down my spine. Reflexively, my hand tightened around my still-stiff cock, and an involuntary gasp escaped my lips. "I'll keep that in mind."

Reaching into my lap, his hand covered mine with a searing touch. I could taste myself on his tongue when his mouth closed over mine.

I wondered what tattoo I'd get next time.

# *Matching Tats*

VIC BRAUNSON HAD a plethora of tattoos inked over much of his muscled bulk—barbed wire wrapped one beefy thigh, a colorful Oriental dragon snaked up one arm. A smattering of Chinese characters peeked out from odd spots: the small of his back, inside his left ankle, behind his right knee, at the base of his neck. Celtic knots crisscrossed his pale skin. His latest piece of art was a black tribal tattoo that curved around his right temple to frame his face. It enhanced his shaved scalp, accentuated his eyebrow piercing, and lent an air of meanness to him that was so incongruous with the man his lover Matt diLorenzo knew. He loved Vic's tattoos. They made him look fierce and cruel, and nothing could've been farther from the truth.

Though Vic had discussed the facial tattoo with Matt before he had it done, seeing it still came as a bit of a shock. It was the first tattoo Vic had gotten in the year and a half since they'd been together, so it was the first tattoo Matt ever saw up close while healing. The glossy black design on his lover's face was the first thing he noticed when he entered the small apartment they shared after a day at the gym, where he worked as a swim instructor. Vic had had the day off from his job as a bus driver for the city and had decided to get the tattoo. He sat at one end of the couch, flipping through television channels in search of something to watch. The tattoo stood out like thick paint, the pale skin around it ruddy with pain. Matt stared at the inked design, fascinated, as he leaned down to plant a quick kiss on Vic's forehead. "So that's it?" he asked.

Vic caught his waist before he could stand and pulled Matt into his lap. With a faint smile, he stared into Matt's dark green eyes and countered, "What do you think?"

"I like." Kneeling on either side of Vic's thick legs, Matt laughed as he sat down on an uncompromising bulge at his lover's crotch. He wriggled his hips a bit, settling himself comfortably on the budding erection. "What's this? Thinking of me, I hope?"

Vic's hands laced together in the small of Matt's back to keep him close. *"Getting inked always turns me on,"* he admitted. Then, pulling Matt to him, Vic sat up to bury his face behind his lover's ear, his breath tickling Matt's skin just below the thick black curls that crowned his head. Silently, he added, *::I was waiting for you before I did anything about it.::*

The thought passed between them easily—to Matt, Vic's mind lay open like a well-read book, the pages curling from overuse, the covers lovingly worn. Every thought Vic had, Matt could read in his mind as if it were his own.

And the mental connection worked both ways; Vic knew everything Matt felt, everything he experienced, everything he thought and saw and did. Yes, they could keep things hidden from each other, but Matt was persistent and hated secrets. Sooner or later, every part of Vic lay bare beneath him, mind and body and soul. Nothing kept them apart.

❖

FOR MATT, THE telepathy ended there. But for Vic, it stretched out to encompass other minds, picking up random thoughts like signals sent from radio stations miles away. Some days it fuzzed out, the connection cloudy; other days it threatened to drive him insane, a million different voices inside his head and none of them his own. The first time he discovered that he had the ability to read others' minds, he thought he *was* going crazy, until he discovered where the power came from.

From Matt. From loving him.

Matt had no special abilities of his own, nothing beyond the psychic meld that spanned between his mind and Vic's, but something in *him* gave Vic a variety of superhuman powers. They passed from one man to the other during sex. Despite his butch appearance, Vic preferred being a submissive bottom in bed, eager to feel Matt move deep within him. Soon after climax, Matt's seed sparked strange super powers in him.

The telepathy had started the first time they'd ever made love, as did the unparalleled super strength that ran through Vic's veins. But the powers didn't end there. Vic had a whole arsenal of comic book antics at his disposal—their positions during sex dictated what power he drew afterward. On his stomach, with Matt driving into him from behind, gave Vic a surplus of kinetic energy that sent sparks flying from his fingertips whenever he touched something electric. A good old blow job, swallowing Matt down, left him with heightened senses that sharpened the world around him, bringing it into vivid, Technicolor detail. And lying on his back on the edge of the bed, with Matt between his legs, holding his knees apart as they fucked, made Vic's skin turn a delicate shade of blue that matched his eyes and kept him confined to the house until the power wore off. *That* was one position they never used again.

The effects of their lovemaking never lingered for long, and a new position quickly replaced one power with the next. Vic never knew what to expect when they tried something new. The powers scared Matt—they put the man he loved in constant danger, giving Vic the ability to help others while putting himself at risk. Every man Matt had ever known intimately had changed once they discovered the powers his semen held for them, and some small part of Matt's mind feared Vic would be the same. Now that he'd finally found a man worth loving, he feared the powers would eventually drive him away.

Patiently Vic had explained that it was *Matt* he loved, not the strange gifts he bestowed; Vic would gladly give them up but didn't want to lose Matt in the process. "I love *you*," he reassured Matt, over and over again. From the moment they met, there'd been a spark between them, something neither could deny. And the fact that Vic had waited patiently for *months* before they moved from friends to lovers said more about the staying power of their relationship than either man could put into words.

Still, Matt rummaged through Vic's mind from time to time, looking through his lover's emotions and feelings as if leafing through a magazine, afraid of what he might find. But Vic stood aside and let him look however long he needed to until he was satisfied that, yes, Vic loved *him*.

*Only* him. The powers be damned.

IN THE LIVING room, on Vic's lap, Matt reached out to touch the new facial tattoo but his lover caught his hand. "Don't," he cautioned, pulling away. "It's healing."

"Why's it all shiny?" Matt wanted to know. He raised his other hand, unconsciously reaching for it a second time, but Vic caught that one, too, and lowered Matt's wrists until he held them against his chest. "Let me feel it."

"Not yet."

"Why's it wet?" Matt asked.

Vic nodded at the end table, where a large jar of petroleum jelly sat, its rectangular lid not quite closed properly. With a laugh, Matt admitted, "And here I thought you just came prepared. That helps it heal?"

"Keeps infection out," Vic explained. He turned his head as Matt leaned closer so he could get a better look.

It was hard to believe the dark ink was now a permanent design etched into the side of his lover's face, but at the same time, Matt found it difficult to remember what Vic's smooth skin had looked like *before* the tattoo. He tried to recall sitting at the dining room table earlier that morning, eating breakfast, just a few hours ago really…but in his memory Vic's face was in profile as his lover mulled over the newspaper. Sitting back, Matt announced, "I want a tattoo."

"What?" Vic laughed. "No, you don't. It hurts like a bitch."

"Can't be *that* bad," Matt reasoned, but Vic laughed again. "You have so many. If it hurts that much, why do you keep getting more?"

Vic shook his head. "They're addicting. If you get one, you'll want another, and another."

With a childish pout, Matt assured him, "I just want one. A little one, even." An idea occurred to him that made his lips spread out in a grin and his eyes widen impishly. "Your name. That's what I want."

The expression on Vic's face was unreadable. He simply stared, and when Matt mentally nudged Vic's mind, he found nothing to indicate what his lover thought of the idea. "Just a small tattoo," Matt tried. He fisted his fingers into the front of Vic's T-shirt, wrists still cuffed by his lover's large hands. "What do you think—"

Vic's gruff voice interrupted him. "Where are you going to put it?"

Matt shrugged. "I don't know."

"Let's find a place," Vic suggested. Then he growled, a playful sound that ignited Matt's blood and, without warning, he wrestled Matt down beside him on the couch.

That lusty rumble in the back of his throat elicited Matt's

laughter. Vic crawled on top of him, snarling and snapping like an angry bear. Beneath him, Matt shrieked in delight as strong hands eased up under the hem of his T-shirt and plucked at the waistband of his shorts. "Vic!" he cried out, laughing as he twisted in his lover's arms.

Warm lips kissed the trembling skin around his navel; inch by inch his shorts slid lower on his hips. When he tried to sit up, blunt teeth nipped at his stomach, tickling him. Unable to catch his breath, Matt giggled soundlessly as Vic ravished him. One image filled both their minds: Vic pinning Matt to the sofa, mouth on any exposed flesh he could find, hands eager as they roamed Matt's body. The erection in Vic's pants now rubbed against the hard cock that tented the front of Matt's swim trunks. Another tug or two on his shorts and his dick would swing free, pointing up at Vic like an accusation. As his lover licked down the faint hairs that led into his shorts, Matt reached out, one hand closing over Vic's ear. The other glanced across the smear of jelly on his fresh tattoo.

They both froze. The jelly felt hot and sticky on Matt's hand. "Oh shit," he murmured. He reached out as if to rub what stuck to his fingers back over the tattoo, but stopped short of touching the spot again. "I'm sorry, Vic. I didn't mean…"

Brushing Matt's hand away, Vic felt his temple. "It's alright." At the worry on Matt's face, he smiled. "Really. I think I'll live."

"I didn't mean to," Matt said again. He tried to touch the tattoo a second time, tentative, but Vic winced and swatted him away. "Does it hurt?"

"Of course it hurts." Vic gave him an incredulous look. "Don't touch it."

"I wasn't going to." But even as he said the words, his hand drifted to the side of Vic's face, unable to stay away.

"Matty," Vic warned. "Stop touching it."

With a wicked grin, Matt reached for the front of Vic's jeans. As he picked at the zipper that hid his lover's erection, the jelly on his hand darkened the denim at Vic's crotch. "Give me something else to play with, then."

"How about keeping your hands to yourself?" Vic countered.

Before Matt could ask what he meant by that, Vic pulled the bottom of Matt's T-shirt up, exposing the smooth skin of his belly and chest. Matt raised his arms as Vic rucked up his shirt, but when it reached his shoulders, Vic stopped. Matt waited, arms draped over his head, blinded by his own shirt. He felt the couch move as Vic stood, but when nothing else happened, he ventured, "Vic?"

His lover spoke directly into his mind. ::*Just a minute, hon. Don't move.*::

Matt heard the solid *thud* of Vic's belt buckle hitting the floor.

"No fair," he pouted, "undressing when I can't see you."

Vic laughed. "You know what it looks like."

Matt pictured Vic towering over him, stiff cock jutting from his groin, thick and veined. The heavy sac of his balls hung low between his legs. Vic's shaved genitals loomed in Matt's mind, larger than life, and Vic laughed again when he picked up on that image. "It's not *that* big."

"It is when I can't see it." Matt started to lower his arms, eager to get things moving between them. "Get this shirt off me already. I can hardly breathe."

Strong hands grabbed the hem of his shirt and tugged. The neck hole slipped over Matt's chin, then his lips, then his nose; he breathed in fresh air as if it were expensive perfume, tingling his senses. "Better?" Vic asked.

Matt raised his hands above his head to indicate he wanted the shirt off completely. His arms were still trapped in sleeves that held tight just below his elbows, and though he could breathe again, he still couldn't see. "All the way please, sir."

"Sir?" Vic teased. His grip tightened on Matt's shirt as he pulled it back, taking Matt with him.

Suddenly Matt found himself being laid down. He wriggled as he was stretched out along the couch. "I can't *see*—"

"You can breathe, right?" Vic asked.

As Matt nodded, he felt large hands tuck the hem of his shirt into the cushions of the couch, trapping his hands and arms and head within the shirt and laying the rest of his body bare to his lover. He sensed Vic leaning over him and he raised his chin, lips puckered, hoping for some contact with the naked man above him. ::*Please,*:: he thought, the word hanging unspoken between them.

An ardent mouth closed over his, claiming him. There was something unfamiliar about the kiss, something exciting, triggered by the fact that Matt kept his eyes open as Vic's tongue licked into him, yet all he saw of his lover was a shadow on the material covering his face. Gentle hands strummed down his arms, tickled over his armpits, rubbed his chest until the tender buds of his nipples hardened beneath the touch. Their kiss deepened as Vic climbed back onto the couch, straddling Matt, his bare buttocks warm against Matt's abdomen, his bent legs cradling Matt's hips. His toes wiggled under Matt's thighs.

Matt could only imagine what a pair they made—himself supine on the couch, Vic above him, kissing him, loving him. Matt felt Vic's hands on his chest but couldn't see them, and the tip of his lover's hard shaft poked at Matt's navel as Vic leaned down for another kiss. All too clearly, Matt could picture Vic's ample ass spread invitingly just inches above the cock that strained the front of Matt's shorts. Thrusting his hips, Matt brushed his crotch against Vic's butt. He whimpered at the momentary touch, the sound lost in Vic's mouth. ::*Please,*:: Matt begged silently. ::*God Vic, please. Just scoot down a little bit, is that asking too much?*::

Inside his mind, his lover laughed. ::*Ask nicely.*::

Matt's imagination conjured up himself as a spoiled kid, close to throwing a tantrum. ::*Please? Please please please*—::

::*Hush.*:: Vic grinned against Matt's mouth, then trailed tiny kisses over his chin and down his throat. Matt gasped at the hot tongue that licked his skin. ::*Now let's see where we should stick this tattoo you want to get.*::

Matt whimpered again; this time the sound bubbled from his throat to escape his lips. Vic's kisses left fire in their wake, burning the imprint of his mouth into Matt's heated skin. When Vic caught a hard nipple between his teeth, Matt's cock jerked in the confines of his shorts, the tip already weeping. "Please," Matt sighed. He wanted this moment to last forever but didn't think he could take much more. And Vic hadn't even gone below his waist yet. "Jesus Christ, Vic, *please.*"

Maddeningly, Vic stopped. Matt bit back a sob. Crossing his arms over Matt's chest, Vic sat back and pressed his ass against Matt's crotch.

Desire and lust blossomed in his groin to settle into a dull ache behind his balls.

"Please what?" Vic wanted to know.

No words could describe just what Matt wanted, so he sent another mental image between them, this one of Vic impaled on Matt's hard cock, hips thrusting his length into his lover's tight, hot core. Every touch, every kiss, every motion boiled down to just the two of them, moving together. One soul in two bodies, seeking release, seeking completion. Made whole.

Scooting down a bit, *finally*, Vic kissed Matt's navel. His tongue swirled around the curl of skin, then his teeth nibbled it playfully. Against Matt's over-sensitized flesh, he breathed, "You read my mind."

"I'm good at that," Matt joked. He felt his lover's dick lying alongside his own and wiggled his hips to draw Vic's attention farther down, where his shorts threatened to cut off the flow of blood pounding in his erection. "Can you help a guy out here, Vic? Take these damn trunks off already, will you?"

Vic sat back. Unable to see his lover, Matt only felt the motion of the sofa beneath him and a sudden chill when Vic's warm body stopped touching his. There was a yank of cloth as Vic pulled Matt's shorts to his knees, and his dick curved up between them. When Vic's hand fisted around his thick shaft, it felt cool and damp, coated with something Matt couldn't immediately place. He moved his arms a bit, trying to pull the shirt up so he could see. "What's that you're smearing on me?"

"Don't move," Vic told him. When Matt ignored him, he spoke directly into Matt's mind. ::*Hon, please. I'm enjoying this.*::

::*At least one of us is,*:: Matt replied. Then it occurred to him—petroleum jelly. *Of course.*

He felt Vic's presence probe inside his head, a gentle sensation that gave him a glimpse of the pleasure trilling through his lover's nude body. For an instant Matt felt the sweet ache that pulsed in Vic's cock and balls, the clench of muscles in his ass at the anticipation building between them, the almost boyish glee that invigorated his blood and couldn't keep the grin from his face.

Grudgingly, he let himself be won over by his lover's enthusiasm. Yes, it *was* a bit exciting, not being able to see or touch Vic. It heightened his senses and made even the slightest brush of skin on skin seem like the first time he'd ever felt another's touch. His flesh tingled where Vic had kissed it; his cock throbbed from the hands that slipped over its slick length.

::*You like this,*:: Vic thought as he thumbed the slit in the tip of Matt's dick. Matt had to bite his lower lip to hold back the orgasm that wanted to tear through him. He wouldn't let it, not yet; he wasn't ready to end this. Vic chuckled as he picked up on Matt's emotions. ::*Don't try to tell me you don't.*::

"Just please," Matt sighed. He bucked into Vic's fists, raising his hips off the couch. "Let me in already, will you?"

"Is that how you ask?" Vic teased.

Matt cried out, exasperated, "Vic!" His lover's laugh infuriated him. "I'm *dying* for you here."

The couch moved as Vic repositioned himself—the hands on Matt's dick worked his length until it felt like a steel shaft wrapped in velvet flesh. The jelly Vic had applied warmed beneath his ministrations; his fists glided along Matt's cock with ease. His fingers picked at Matt's cockhead once, twice, tiny pinches that made him gasp and writhe on the couch. *God,* he thought, his mind a blur. *Jesus* and *please* and *Vic oh Vic oh God*

*Vic...*the words ran together in his head, a litany that surpassed language and soared into the realm of pure sensation. One word resonated as Vic fondled him—::*Yes.*::

Suddenly heavy knees sank to the couch on either side of Matt's thighs, and large, tight buttocks pressed against the tip of his dick. He thrust up and felt hot flesh take him in, Vic's tight hole puckering around his dick as he eased inside. They fit together like clockwork, bodies meshing like well-worn gears, in a rhythm as old as time itself. As Vic sat down on Matt, taking the full length into him, he opened his mind to his lover, letting his emotions and passion pour into Matt's body to mingle with his own lustful desire.

In his mind Matt could see what Vic saw—himself on the couch, chest bare, Vic straddling his hips as Matt moved deep within his lover. Vic leaned back against the arm of the couch. One hand danced over Matt's lower belly, smearing it with petroleum jelly, as the other worked his own erection, pressing it into the dark kinked curls at Matt's groin, rubbing the hard length between his hand and Matt's body. Deep inside him, strong muscles worked at Matt's cock, massaging it. Slowly, oh *God,* so slowly, Vic moved above him, bringing him to release.

When Matt finally came, it was in a quick rush that raised his hips off the sofa, driving him deeper into his lover. He cried out Vic's name, and God's, and whatever else came to mind as the sexual tension and pressure building in him climaxed. As his seed shot into Vic, he felt hot juices slick his abdomen. Vic trailed a hand through his own cum, then touched one spunk-covered finger to Matt's lips. Matt closed his mouth around the offering, suckling at Vic's fingertip. He only released it when his lover lay down over him to replace that finger with his own lips. "Love you," Vic murmured into Matt. "You still want that tattoo?"

"What?" Matt asked, breathless. Were they still talking about that? With a tug at the shirt pinning him down, he added, "Let me hold you."

When Vic pried the T-shirt off over his head, Matt had to

blink at the sudden light. He felt like a newborn babe in a strange new world. Vic released one arm, then the other, then cradled Matt to his chest. Reaching behind him, he snagged an afghan off the back of the couch and draped it over them both. When he tried to slide to one side, though, Matt held him fast above him. He didn't want to lose the warmth of Vic's body against his, and he wasn't ready to pull out from his lover just yet. Vic protested, "I'm a bit heavy—"

Matt cut off his words with a kiss. *::Hush,::* he replied. *::You're right where I want you.::*

MAYBE IT WAS Vic's healing tattoo, or Matt's talk of getting inked, or just a lucky coincidence. Whatever the reason, their bout of lovemaking on the sofa triggered a new and strange power in Vic, more supernatural than superhuman. On its own accord, his skin began to display spontaneous tattoos. Odd designs darkened various parts of his body, appearing on his skin as if welling up from within. They shone wetly for a few minutes, then disappeared—haikus in kanji letters written out across his stomach, a complicated Möbius strip that spanned his chest, a series of elaborate sand castles that sprang up on his back and then faded as if washed away by an invisible tide. Tiny tribal markings appeared on Vic's face, framing his lips and goatee, before dissolving away. The fake tattoos played around the edges of his real ones, giving his skin a constantly shifting appearance. It was beautiful to watch, and Matt stared at the images that arose on his lover's body, fascinated by the power he'd inadvertently given him.

But over the next few days, the ability faded—they all did in time. The designs appearing on Vic's flesh grew fainter by the hour, black paling into a worn-out blue, intricacies falling apart into simple line drawings, then stick figures, then nothing. By the end of the week, the only tattoos on Vic's body were the ones he'd paid to have put there. The ink on his face healed nicely, with little scabbing. Whenever Matt looked at it, he thought again about getting his own tattoo.

"Just a little one," he told Vic one morning at breakfast. He kept bringing it up, not so much because he wanted his lover's permission, because he knew Vic wouldn't mind, but because he wanted his lover to help talk him into it. Not that he was *afraid*, really. Just…uncertain. He wanted a tattoo, he *did*. It was the needles and the thought of pain, no matter how temporary, that gave him pause. "Your initials maybe. What do you think?"

It was becoming a familiar discussion, one Vic wouldn't let himself be drawn into for long. He wanted Matt to make the decision—he'd support it, of course, but he wouldn't make it for him. He *couldn't*. He kept pushing that thought into Matt's mind in the hopes that it would stick there, but Matt was stubborn and kept pressing Vic for a more definite answer. With a shrug, Vic reminded him, "It's permanent, Matty. If you're sure…"

Matt grabbed his lover's hand in both of his. "*This* is permanent. *We're* permanent. I've never been more sure of anything in my life."

What started as three little letters grew into a heart with Vic's initials inside, and if Matt was serious about it, then Vic wanted one, too. And if they were getting matching tats, they needed to find a spot to suit them both, which crossed off anywhere Vic already had an image inked into his skin. Matt suggested an ankle, but Vic told him it would hurt more, right on the bone. When Matt stood and turned to slap his butt, only half teasing, Vic vetoed that, too. "No one's touching your ass but me," he growled.

Eventually they decided on the fleshy upper area of their right arms. "When do you want to go get it done?" was Vic's next question.

Matt didn't have an answer for that. "Soon," he assured his lover. Silently he added, *Just as soon as I work up the courage to do it, or hell, as soon as I get drunk enough…*

Picking up that thought, Vic pressed Matt's hand to his mouth and kissed his knuckles. "We don't have to do this," he started.

But Matt shook his head, adamant. "We will."

The idea had taken root in his mind. He wouldn't let himself back down.

VIC DIDN'T MENTION the tattoo again, but Matt couldn't stop worrying over it. What it would look like, what colors he'd use. He spent too many hours at the gym Googling tattoo designs online when he was supposed to be working. Finally he settled for a red heart, outlined in black, with Vic's initials inked in a white banner across the center. One evening, when the two of them lay in bed, the sheets entwined around their naked bodies, Matt showed the design to his lover. Vic simply said, "I'm sure Big Man can do this."

"Big Man?" Matt asked. "Who's that?"

"Guy who does my tats." Vic set the piece of paper on his bedside table, then ruffled his lover's hair. "So I guess we're still on with this?"

Reaching across Vic's wide chest, Matt snagged the paper from the table and looked it over again. "Of course." He held the paper up to his shoulder, then leaned against Vic to show his lover. "What do you think? You like it?"

For a long moment, Vic stared at the design. Growing nervous, Matt mentally prodded, ::*Vic? Well?*::

A sudden rush of lust poured into Matt, staggering him. With a shaky laugh, Matt asked, "What's that for?"

"Tattoos turn me on," Vic admitted. His eyes gleamed with an inner heat, and his lips curved in a wicked grin. "I bought you something."

"What?" Matt rolled back to his side of the bed and deposited the paper with his tattoo design on it on his own bedside table. Then he turned to Vic like an excited little boy. "When did you get it?"

With a laugh, Vic opened the drawer on the table next to him. Whatever he extracted hid easily in his large hands. Matt tugged at his elbow, eager to see the gift. "What is it?"

Vic opened his hands and held out a small booklet of temporary tattoos. Matt stared at them, confused. "Why'd you get these?" he asked, taking the booklet from Vic. He flipped through it—the tattoos were black, and all of the same Chinese character. Some were large, the size of his palm; some were tiny little rows of the same symbol, written over and over again. Matt turned the booklet over and saw the design printed on the cover, the word *LOVE* written beneath it. He laughed. "How sweet. This doesn't change my mind, though. I still want that damn heart."

"This is just for fun," Vic told him. Taking the booklet, he tore out the first page, then handed the rest to Matt. "There are some instructions on the back. Read them to me. Where do you want this one?"

Laying back against the pillows, Matt pulled down the bed sheets to expose his hip. "Here?" he asked, pointing to a flat spot low on his belly. His stomach fluttered when Vic touched it. "How does it stick to the skin?"

"Read the directions," Vic said again.

Matt frowned at the booklet, trying to read the fine print typed on the back cover. "Apply to clean, damp skin—"

A warm tongue licked the spot Matt chose. The sensation, so sudden and unexpected, ignited his blood and tented the sheet covering his crotch. If *that* was how they were going to play, Matt could think of a dozen *other* places to put that tattoo. With a shaky laugh, he pulled the sheets over an inch closer to his groin and pointed again. "Maybe here instead."

Vic's tongue darted out to lick that place, too. Dropping the book of temporary tattoos, Matt gripped his hard cock through the sheets and gasped. As he watched, Vic nosed the sheet aside, his tongue licking beneath the fabric to wet down kinked curls. He found the root of Matt's shaft, licked beneath it to taste his fuzzy nuts, then leaned in to close his mouth around the base of Matt's erection. "God," Matt sighed.

Vic's breath tickled Matt's saliva slicked skin. "Well?" he asked. "What next?"

Matt fumbled for the booklet. "Um…" The words swam before him, unreadable. His nerves buzzed, his mind a blur— Vic's body was a familiar weight against his legs, and Matt couldn't concentrate on the fine print with his lover's tongue lapping his hip like a grooming cat. He wanted that tongue beneath the sheet again, around his dick. Could they put the tattoo there?

*::Matty.::* Vic nudged him with his mind, a loving touch. Aloud he asked, "What's next?"

"Press tattoo onto skin." Matt watched Vic position the tattoo on his hip, then press it down with one heavy hand. "Um, wet the back of the tat—"

Vic licked out again, this time wetting the paper stuck to Matt's hip. His tongue swirled over the white paper, dampening it, until it seemed to dissolve into Matt's skin. The black ink of the tattoo showed through the transparent paper in dark contrast to Matt's pale skin. When it was good and wet, Vic glanced up at Matt, who breathed, "Peel it off carefully."

With gentle fingers, Vic peeled the paper backing away, leaving the dark tattoo in its place. Tentatively Matt touched it, smoothed it down. Reaching for the tattoo booklet, Vic asked, "Where do you want the next one?"

Matt imagined himself on his stomach, ass in the air, as Vic licked another tattoo onto the tender flesh of his inner thigh, just below his buttocks. Catching that thought, Vic's grin widened. "Flip over, lover boy."

The sheets tangled around Matt's legs as he hurried to comply.

❖

TALKING ABOUT GETTING a tattoo and actually sitting in the parlor next in line turned out to be two completely different things, Matt discovered.

The Saturday before Labor Day, he woke up convinced that if he didn't get the damn tattoo today, right now, this *instant*, he'd chicken out and never go through with it. Impatiently he paced the small kitchen and circled the dining room table where Vic sat nursing a cup of coffee, trying to wake up. "Sit down, will you?" his lover grumbled. He nudged the chair beside him to block Matt's path. With a huff, Matt fell into the chair, arms crossed, one leg jiggling so hard, it shook the table. Vic placed a hand on Matt's knee to still it. "The place doesn't even open until noon."

Somehow Matt managed to make it that long, but nervousness churned his stomach and he didn't dare eat any lunch, for fear he wouldn't keep it down. By the time they entered the tattoo parlor, his mind whirled out in a sort of euphoric rush. This was what he wanted to do, he *knew* it. No regrets.

But doubt crept in when he met the tattoo artist, a scrawny guy Vic introduced as Big Man, whose colorful shirt with its long sleeves turned out to be one large tattoo that covered him from neck to waist, shoulder to shoulder, and down each arm to stop at his wrists. He had a wiry beard he wore twisted in a braid, and a broken front tooth that looked like a fang when he grinned. As he led them down a dingy hallway, Matt's apprehension grew with each step.

The hallway ended at a small room that looked surgically clean, despite the many posters gracing the walls of heavily tattooed, big-breasted women in various states of undress. A hulking machine sat in one corner; trays of sterile needles and small pots of ink lined the available counter space. Matt watched with dreadful fascination as Big Man opened a clean set of needles and began attaching them to the tattoo machine. When he unwrapped an unused disposable razor, Matt's voice crept up an octave. "What's that for?"

Vic's hand touched Matt's hip. "Relax," his lover murmured. "You're gonna get yourself all worked up before anything even happens." Slipping his arm around Matt's waist, Vic pulled him into a quick, one-arm embrace. He nosed aside Matt's thick black curls to whisper into his ear, "You sure you want to go through with this?"

"It was *my* idea," Matt reminded him. If Vic could withstand the momentary discomfort of getting a tattoo then damn it, Matt could, too. Speaking directly into his lover's mind, he asked, ::*It doesn't hurt for too long, right?*::

Vic's reply was a kiss on his ear, and the mental assurance, ::*You'll be fine.*::

What looked like a dentist's chair took up most of the room—Vic dropped into it without waiting to be asked. There was a stool for Big Man, who wheeled in a second one for Matt. As he sat down, trying to look everywhere at once, he felt a warm hand cover his and glanced at Vic, only to find a smoldering look in his lover's eyes. With a self-conscious grin, Matt asked, "What?"

Vic's gaze flickered to Big Man, who studiously ignored them as he filled tiny cups with red and black ink. Still, Vic spoke to Matt through their psychic connection, well aware of their audience. ::*I never thought I'd see you in a place like this,*:: he admitted silently. With a tug on Matt's hand, he rolled his lover's stool closer. His fingers slipped into Matt's lap to poke at the front of his crotch. Raw lust rushed over Matt like the tide, drowning him in Vic's passion. In the confines of his pants, Matt's cock twitched to life as Vic's gruff voice filled his mind. ::*Turns me on. Damn, I want you.*::

Matt laughed as he ran a nervous hand through his hair. Vic's middle finger traced the curve of his zipper, pressing into the slight erection hidden in Matt's jeans. ::*Hold that thought,*:: Matt told him. ::*When we're done here—*::

A few feet away, Big Man cleared his throat to remind them

they weren't alone. "We about ready?" he asked, not looking in their direction.

Vic gave Matt a salacious wink. "Oh, yeah."

A dull blush crept into Matt's face, heating his cheeks, but he caught Vic's hand in both of his and pressed his lover's knuckles to his lips for a quick kiss before scooting out of the way. Perched on the edge of his stool, he watched, wide-eyed, as Big Man prepped Vic for the tattoo.

First he cleaned a spot on Vic's arm, daubing the skin with alcohol and some green, foaming mess that squirted out of a bottle like hairspray. The disposable razor scraped uselessly over already bald skin. Then he applied what looked like a temporary tattoo, rubbing it onto Vic's shoulder like a template to guide him during the tattoo process. Matt thought of his own temporary tats, just now beginning to flake off. A line of Chinese characters still encircled his dick just below its plum-like head; whenever he tried to rub them away, he ended up jerking off instead. And this morning in the shower, he'd scratched below his right buttock and came away with black ink under his fingernails. He could still remember the way Vic's tongue had felt as his lover pressed the tattoo into his skin.

Vic's dark gaze flickered past Big Man. "I know what you're thinking," he teased.

Before Matt could reply, Big Man uncapped a felt-tip marker to trace the outline of the heart, then leaned in to write. "What are the initials again?"

Together Matt and Vic both said, "*M, R, D.*" As Big Man began to write, Matt clarified, "*D* as in *David.*"

Big Man nodded. Sitting back, he turned Vic's arm toward Matt for his approval. The sight of his initials on his lover's skin excited him. "That's it," he sighed. He reached out for the heart but pulled back before touching the area and ruining the image. "It looks great."

He couldn't wait for his own turn in the chair, but the noise the tattoo machine made when Big Man started it up almost changed his mind. High and piercing, a thousand times worse than a dentist's drill, the constant buzz of the needles made Matt's stomach flip. When Big Man touched the needle to Vic's shoulder, the grimace that flickered over his lover's face terrified Matt. *::It hurts, doesn't it?::*

Vic raised one eyebrow and pressed his lips together. Following Matt's lead, he used their mental connection to speak. *::Of course it hurts.::*

Taking a deep breath, Matt punched his fists into his thighs to force himself to calm down. But Vic was the strongest man he knew, even without the super strength Matt's semen gave him. If *Vic* flinched at the needle, how would Matt react? *Please don't let me scream,* he prayed as he watched Big Man retrace the heart drawn onto Vic's arm. The first bright drops of blood began to well up from his lover's irritated skin. *I'll bite my tongue in half if I have to but God, please don't let me scream like a girl.*

Vic heard that thought loud and clear. Glancing over in concern, he asked, "You doing okay, Matty?"

"Is it supposed to bleed so much?" Matt asked, unable to keep the nervousness from his voice.

"I'm a free bleeder," Vic answered. The way he said it, so nonchalant, told Matt this was nothing new. He nodded weakly, but couldn't tear his gaze from the needle or the blood that pinked Vic's skin when Big Man wiped it away from the tattoo.

FIFTEEN MINUTES LATER, Big Man turned off the tattoo machine. Matt's ears continued to ring, as if the noise itself had been tattooed into his brain. With another squirt of the antibacterial liquid, Big Man cleaned Vic's latest tattoo with a paper towel. Matt watched the colored skin distend, the image moving as Big Man rubbed over it with short, brusque motions. When Big Man turned away, Matt got a clear view of the red heart, the white banner a vivid contrast, the tiny black letters inside, *his*

initials, a part of him forever emblazoned on his lover's body.

As he watched, beads of blood bubbled up through the ink like stigmata. Matt felt an uneasy pressure rise in him at the sight, a sickness like the tide threatening to drag him under. His face burned; when he touched his cheeks, his fingers felt like ice. Who was he kidding? He didn't like seeing himself bleed over a paper cut, loathed a shaving nick, and here he was about to get a *tattoo*? Was he *crazy*?

Matt rose to his feet, his mind in turmoil. He didn't know if he could go through with it, didn't know if he *wanted* to, but one thing was sure…"I've got to go."

Big Man looked up from covering Vic's new tattoo with medical gauze. "Go where?" Vic asked with a frown. "You're next, babe."

Anxiety twisted Matt's stomach, strangling the words trapped in his throat. "I…I can't." His mouth tried to smile as he frowned, and he wiped a hand across his face as he drew in a shuddery breath. The confusion in Vic's eyes was painful to see. ::*I'm sorry*,:: Matt thought. Remembering Big Man, he spoke out loud, hating the small, wounded voice that came from his lips. "I'm sorry. I'm…I think I'm going to be sick."

He hit the door at a dead run. Behind him, he heard Big Man call out, "Bathroom's on the right! If he spews in the hall—"

"Give him a minute," Vic said. "He'll be fine." His thoughts chased after Matt, seeking a similar reassurance. ::*Right?*::

::*God*,:: Matt shot back. In the dim hallway he found a door-knob that opened beneath his touch and he fell into a dark room, hands fumbling along the wall for the switch. Above, one bare bulb flashed to life, illuminating a small closet that barely held an old cracked toilet and low sink. Slamming the door shut behind him, Matt twisted the spigot and splashed bracing water onto his face.

*Jesus.*

He couldn't do this, couldn't go through with it. He was a fucking *wimp*. What would Vic think of him now? ::*I'm so sorry*—::

Vic's soothing presence filled his mind. ::*Calm down, Matty.*::

The water stung his face like ice. Rivulets ran down his neck, dampening his T-shirt. Slowly the urgent need to vomit passed, leaving him weak and dizzy. Calm, yes, he was calm. Alone in the cramped bathroom, he felt his lover's arms around him, heard tender words nuzzled into his head. ::*Calm.*:: Vic's soft whispers overpowered the needles' piercing buzz, and when Matt closed his eyes, it was his lover's face he saw, not the swell of blood on Vic's fresh tattoo. Taking a deep breath to steady himself, he let Vic's powerful psyche quell the turmoil that raged within him. Maybe it wouldn't be *too* bad. If Vic could do it…

A heavy hand knocked on the door to the bathroom. Before Matt could answer, he heard his lover's gruff voice against the wood. "You in there, Matty?"

"I'll be right out," Matt called.

The knock came again, and this time the doorknob turned, insistent. "Let me in."

Matt reached over and turned the knob, unlocking the door. As Vic entered the tiny bathroom, Matt crossed his arms in front of his chest, hugging himself against the far wall to make room for his lover. He felt like a recalcitrant child waiting to be chastised. Vic didn't have to point out that this was his own idea; Matt was well aware of that little fact. Somehow, it made the whole situation that much worse. He looked weak and stupid, yes, and he couldn't raise his gaze to meet his lover's, so sure of the disappointment he'd see there.

But when Vic spoke, there was only soft kindness in his voice. "Matty, it's okay."

His words touched Matt deep inside, unraveling the frenzied ball of emotions that had wound up in him. Taking his elbow, Vic pulled him closer, and Matt let himself open up to his lover's embrace. "I'm a wuss," he mumbled as his arms found their way around Vic's broad waist. "This was my idea in the first place and now I can't do it. I just can't."

"Shhh," Vic murmured against his neck. One hand rubbed

Matt's back in a soothing gesture. "You don't have to if you don't want to."

Matt sighed. "I *do*, that's just it. But it'll hurt—"

"It'll sting a bit," his lover conceded.

Matt tried again. "It'll bleed."

Vic nodded. "It might."

Silently Matt pointed out, ::*You're not helping here.*::

Leaning back against the sink, Vic hugged Matt to him. When he shifted his feet apart, Matt fit comfortably between his legs, their bellies flat against each other, an unmistakable bulge pressing into Matt's crotch. With a sly smile, Matt thrust his hips against Vic's and murmured, "What's this?"

"I told you it turned me on," Vic said with a laugh, "seeing you in a place like this."

His folded hands rested comfortably on Matt's butt; their familiar, heavy weight helped calm him. Leaning back in Vic's embrace, Matt picked at the buttons on his lover's sleeveless shirt and pouted. "There's nothing sexy about me being scared."

"You don't look scared," Vic countered. He kissed Matt's temple, his cheek, his chin, then ducked his head to force Matt to look at him. "You look amazing," he murmured. "You look strong and confident and so damn sure of yourself. That's the guy I love. The guy who does what he says he's going to do. Who makes up his mind and sticks with it. Who isn't afraid of shit, where's he hiding now?"

With a faint smile, Matt admitted, "I think I left him at home. If I could just stop *thinking* already and just get in there and *do* it—"

Vic silenced him with a kiss that lingered on his mouth. Matt opened to him, letting him in. The soft press of lips and insistent tongue sent shivers down his spine, quickening his blood and weakening his knees. Vic pulled back just enough to sigh into him, "You need a distraction."

"This works," Matt managed before Vic chased his words away with a lick of his tongue. His hands slipped down to cradle

Matt's buttocks, squeezing his firm ass through jeans that suddenly chafed over-sensitized skin. Then, one hand holding him close, the other trailed over his hip to rub at the front of his crotch. Vic fingered the curve of Matt's zipper, his nail *pop pop popping* over the tiny metal teeth as his hidden cock stiffened beneath the touch. Matt's own hands fisted in Vic's shirt, pulling his lover closer as their kiss deepened.

Between them, Vic thumbed open the fly on Matt's jeans. The zipper parted—his fingers eased into the front of Matt's briefs, tickled through cottony hair, stroked the hard, thick shaft that jumped at his touch. "Please," Matt moaned, taking a step back. He found himself up against the wall as the small bathroom closed in around them and everything else disappeared—everything that wasn't Vic before him, the hands down his pants, the mouth on his.

Without a word his lover sank to the floor, tugging Matt's jeans and briefs down with him in one swift motion. Matt's swollen erection swung free, rising to meet the eager mouth that closed over his bulbous cockhead with a sweet kiss. Vic's mouth seared Matt's flesh, his tongue circling the tender tip of his dick before taking the full length in. Arching away from the wall, Matt thrust into his lover, legs trembling at the sensations that flooded his body. The hot mouth suckling, loving him; the hand between his legs, massaging his balls like dice in his lover's palm. One long finger stretched across the hidden flesh between his legs to tickle the puckered skin of his ass.

Vic's other hand strummed Matt's lower belly, pushing the T-shirt he wore out of the way as he fondled Matt's navel. Every inch of Matt's body fluttered at the touch. His blood raced, pounding in his chest, his temples, his dick, tingling his nerves, enflaming his senses. "Please," he gasped, and "yes," and "God, Vic, yes, *yes.*" Matt gripped Vic's hand tight, then rubbed over his lover's shaved scalp, plucked at his ears, held his head as he fucked into the willing mouth. He quivered from the loving ministrations, the hands on his body, the mouth and tongue and lips that guided him to release.

With long strokes of his tongue, Vic worshipped Matt's cock. On his knees now, he concentrated on the full length of Matt's erection, beginning at the tip and swirling down to the thick base, buried in musky curls. His saliva slicked down Matt's dark pubic hair, coated his throbbing balls, cooled the heated skin behind them that Vic licked out to taste. "God," Matt sobbed. His body was on fire, ignited by his lover, a pyre burning bright, fueled by mutual desire.

Suddenly Vic stood and turned, dropping his own jeans to the floor to present the twin pale mounds of his buttocks. "Fuck me, Matty," he growled as he gripped the sink in both hands, feet spread apart as wide as they'd go with the jeans cuffing his ankles. "Fuck me hard. You know how I like it."

Matt didn't have to be asked twice. Brushing the hem of Vic's shirt up out of the way, Matt held his lover's hips as he worked the tip of his dick between the round cheeks of Vic's ass. His lover gasped and pushed back against him at the same moment Matt thrust into his hot center; they met in a clash of skin and sweat, Matt fisting the fabric of Vic's shirt, Vic's knuckles as white as the porcelain sink he clung to. They moved together in an ancient rhythm, fast and rough, Vic bucking as Matt drove into him, seeking release.

The connection they shared opened like floodgates, and a myriad of emotions tumbled between them. They shared every aspect of the deed—Matt felt his own cock bump his prostate as he thrust into Vic, and knew that Vic's swollen glans throbbed as if inside his own tight ass. They came simultaneously, an orgasmic rush that tore through them both, ratcheting their emotions into a realm of pure sensation, beyond thought and fear, beyond words. Burrowed deep inside Vic, Matt wrapped his arms around his lover's waist and leaned against him, a fierce hug that seemed to be all that held the both of them upright. "Oh God," he sighed into the damp skin along the back of Vic's neck. "I love you."

One hand covered Matt's. Vic's sphincters, still clenched, held the wilting cock within him. When he spoke, his voice was thick with emotion. "I won't think anything less of you if you can't go through with this—"

"I can."

The words slipped out unbidden, and Matt kissed his lover's shoulder as if to punctuate his assent. He *needed* that tattoo now, if only to burn *this* moment into his memory forever, a testament to the love they shared. His voice sounded strong and sure, no longer laced with doubt. "I will, right now, before I can change my mind."

But he didn't relax his grip around Vic's waist, and neither moved, unwilling to spoil the sudden intimacy that enveloped them. When Matt finally loosened his arms, Vic held onto his wrist to keep him close. "Big Man," Matt started.

In the mirror above the sink, Vic met Matt's gaze. He clenched his buttocks, renewing Matt's interest. "Let him wait."

WHEN THEY RETURNED, Matt entered the room first, Vic's hand held fast in his. Big Man's gaze dropped to those entwined hands, then raised to meet Vic's stern eyes. From the look on his face, Matt suspected Big Man knew about their tryst in the bathroom, but he didn't say a word as Matt dropped into the tattooing chair. Ignoring the second stool, Vic sank down to sit on the edge of Matt's chair. "This cool with you?" he asked the tattoo artist.

Big Man shrugged. "Just don't move," he cautioned in a weary voice that said he'd seen it all. "I don't want to fuck up the art."

As Big Man prepped his ink, Matt rolled his shirt sleeve up over his shoulder. One of Vic's large hands rested easily on his thigh, comforting him. His lover's voice filled him inside when Vic telepathically reassured him, ::*You'll be fine.*::

With a wan smile, Matt took a deep breath and held it. He closed his eyes, trying to center himself. *Don't think about the pain*, his mind whispered. *Don't think about anything if you can help it. Fifteen minutes and it'll all be over. That's not too long for something that will last a lifetime, is it?*

And then Vic was there, his presence warming Matt's body as if his lover lay above him. Matt felt Vic's heart beat in time with his own, felt his lover's pulse through his own veins, saw himself through his lover's eyes. He looked fearless and strong. He could do this. He *would*.

The first spritz of soapy liquid startled him, so cold against his overheated skin. He opened his eyes and saw Vic frowning at the bandage that covered his own new tattoo. As Big Man ran the straight-edge razor over his upper arm, Matt asked, "What's the matter?"

"It itches," Vic replied. He scratched at the bandage hard enough to tear the medical tape away from his skin. Smoothing it back down, he told Matt, "Usually only bothers me later, when it's healing."

Now Big Man pressed the template onto Matt's flesh. His impersonal manner was incongruous with the loving way Vic had applied the temporary tattoos earlier. When Big Man retraced the outline of the tattoo, the pen tickled Matt's damp skin. He remembered the feel of Vic's tongue on his body, licking the tattoos into place, and he sent that memory into Vic's mind, a wicked grin already toying at the edges of his lips. ::*Remember*—::

A flash of intense pain flared through him and was gone. He jolted, but Big Man held his shoulder in an uncompromising grip that prevented him from moving. "Stop," the tattoo artist warned.

"Vic?" Matt reached out for his lover, but Vic's concentration was on the bandage and the piercing itch beneath it—the source of the pain Matt felt ricochet through him. He watched in disbelief as Vic ripped the bandage aside to scratch across the surface of his new tattoo. "God, Vic, don't *do* that! You'll ruin it…"

But the tattoo beneath the bandage no longer looked fresh and bloody. The ink had dried, the skin healed. Matt's initials looked as if they'd been touched up recently—the colors were vivid and bright—but there were no scabs on the tattoo, nothing to indicate that it had just been carved into his arm. It looked *nothing* like Vic's facial tattoo had when healing.

Big Man shook Matt's arm to get his attention. "Initials?" he asked, his voice brusque. "Come on, guys. I ain't got all day. What—"

"*V, S, B,*" Vic told him. He ran his hand over the tattoo and flinched. Matt could pick up some residual pain deep in his lover's muscles but nothing more. With a sardonic twist of his lips, Vic mused, ::*Now we know what position gives me healing powers.*::

Suddenly the tattoo machine hummed to life. Matt tensed, fingers digging into the soft arms of the chair. "Relax," Big Man told him as he positioned the buzzing needles near Matt's shoulder. "It'll hurt more if you don't."

Matt felt Vic pry his hand off the arm of the chair. He folded Matt's fingers into his own palm. A warmth spread through them at the touch, a golden glow that seemed to pour from Vic's hand into Matt's, then move along his wrist, up his arm. Strength and love wove through him, encasing him in an armor that kept the rest of the world at bay. When the needles touched his skin, Matt heard their insistent *whirr* but barely felt their bite. Vic's newfound healing power managed to drive the pain away.

Matt dared to peek at the tattoo taking shape on his arm. The spots already inked in stood out glossy against the faded temporary tattoo, but there was no blood. No scabbing, no wound. The healing ability Matt had unwittingly transferred to Vic during sex flowed back into him easily at his lover's touch. ::*This isn't so bad,*:: he thought.

The sharp look Vic threw at him made him grin. ::*Oh yeah, easy for you to say.*::

Puckering his lips together, Matt blew his lover a kiss and

amended, ::*When we get home, I'll thank you properly.*::

A distracting image rose unbidden in Matt's head—himself on the floor of their living room, Vic in front of him. Both naked. He sent the thought to his lover, then played the scene out between them like a movie. In their minds, Matt stretched his legs out between Vic's. His long feet glistened with lotion, and they left slick trails along Vic's legs as they rubbed over his knees and up his lover's inner thighs.

Inside their heads, Vic watched Matt plant one foot against his shaved balls, fitting the sac perfectly into the arch of his sole. His toes wiggled, exciting Vic's dick, the nails skimming over his skin with a dry sound. The other foot curled down the length of Vic's dick.

Spreading his legs wider, Vic slouched down to allow Matt full access to his genitalia. Matt's large feet rubbed over his balls and dick, squeezing him, kneading him, playing with him as they both grew more aroused by the moment. Steepling his long toes over Vic's erection, Matt stroked the hard length with only the soles of his feet. Then he caught Vic's shaft between two toes and strummed from tip to base in one smooth stroke. His toes massaged Vic's hairless crotch, pressing into him when his hips rose off the ground. With one heel against his balls, Matt fondled his lover with both feet, toes tickling his cockhead and curving delicately around his shaft...

A sudden silence spawned around them—it took a moment for Matt to realize the tattoo machine had been turned off. He opened his eyes to find Big Man wiping the new tattoo on his arm with a paper towel but there was no blood, nothing to wipe away. "Wow." With a squeeze of Vic's hand, Matt turned his arm to show his lover the tattoo. "Check this out, hon."

Vic stared, jaws slack, eyes hooded with lust. The front of his jeans strained beneath an erection roused by Matt's sexy, sinful thoughts. He had a foot fetish, Matt knew, and apparently the thought of a foot-job seemed to incapacitate him. "Vic?"

Vic cleared his throat, shook his head, ran a hand over the

top of his bald scalp and frowned at the tattoo as he struggled to move from the realm of emotion back to the land of the living. "Looks good," he grumbled, his voice like thunder in the small room. "Real good, Matty. You like it?"

Before Matt could respond, Vic surged to his feet, already digging out his wallet. "How much we owe you?" Pulling out a hundred dollar bill, he folded it into Big Man's fist. "This should cover it. Two medium tats are what, forty each? Plus tax, keep the change. Real good job, man. Thanks a lot."

Vic grabbed Matt's arm and hauled him to his feet. As he led the way from the room, Matt laughed. "Vic, wait…"

His lover's mind opened to his, a whirl of blinding lust and red-hot passion sizzling in him. ::*Can't wait. I need you. Now.*::

Matt's laughter chased them from the tattoo parlor as the rest of the afternoon stretched out ahead like a promise.

*Author's Note:* To read more about the super-powered relationship shared between Vic and Matt, visit vic-and-matt.com.

# *Mojo's Mojo*

WEDNESDAY EVENING, MY last client runs a little late. Tattoo 804 closes at eight o'clock, but I'm doing the final fill work on a pin-up style cowgirl riding a large spermatozoon as if it were a bucking bronco. I'm not one to judge—I'll ink anything on anyone if they're old enough and can pay me to do it. I like my work, and while drawing cowgirls riding giant sperm isn't exactly my idea of fine art, it pays the rent. A large job like this sets the customer back a cool three hundred, and the way this parlor operates, almost of it goes straight into my pocket.

It doesn't matter what the tattoo is *of*, really—I take pride in crisp lines and smooth fades, and clean blends where the colors meet. When I'm satisfied with the quality of my work, I wipe the tattoo clean with antiseptic soap and snap a quick picture of it on my iPhone. This one's definitely going on my Facebook page. As I start covering it with clear plastic wrap, a shadow crosses behind me and I glance back at Mojo, who owns the booth next to mine. "That shit's tight, man," he tells me.

I nod to acknowledge the complement. The customer half-turns—the tattoo's on her back so she can't really see it—and asks Mojo, "So it looks all right?"

"Gorgeous," he says, leaning past me to take a closer look.

I can faintly smell the lingering remnants of his aftershave, something musky that makes me feel warm inside. I love that scent—most of the time I catch whiffs of it throughout the day as he works beside me. It does wicked things to my scrotum.

Clapping a hand on my back, Mojo tells my client, "Wray's one of the best in Richmond. He did a kick-ass job on you."

As I tape the plastic wrap into place, I joke, "He's only saying that because he wants something."

The hand resting heavily on my shoulder takes a swipe at my head. I duck and grin up at him. Mojo's not really what you'd call sexy to look at—he's a little on the large side, with broad shoulders and hips that must've made him the one to beat on the football field back in high school. That was easily fifteen years ago, and the once firm muscles have begun to get a soft look about them. He has a fierce grip, though, and can arm wrestle anyone under the table, though he has the lightest touch of any tattoo artist I know. You'd never guess it looking at him, but his tattoos rarely bruise or crust up like some people's I could mention, and his filigree work is so damn delicate. Ladies love to book appointments with him—he does killer tramp stamps and intricate lettering, and flirts with everyone.

Literally, *everyone*.

When I began working at the 804, I thought he was coming onto *me* and by the end of my first night, I was half in love with the guy. Then I found out he has a girlfriend, and any lustful notions I might've harbored about the two of us getting freaky in my car after work disappeared.

Mojo's charm is in his personality. He has an easy laugh I've started to hear in my sleep and a way of smiling with his whole face that makes his warm hazel eyes crinkle into half-moons when he's pleased. God, I'd do anything to see them crinkle my way. I joke and kid with Mojo constantly, trying to one-up myself to keep him interested in me. Girlfriend or not, the guy *does* flirt with me along with everyone else. I keep telling myself it's just a matter of time before he looks at me and wonders, hmm…

My client slips me a twenty dollar bill as a tip and checks out the tattoo in the mirror beside my booth before pulling down the back of her shirt. "Thanks, guys," she says, as if Mojo somehow helped out.

He watches the sway of her hips as she pushes through the front door, and I watch him. When I first started here, I would've laughed if someone suggested I might one day find a guy like him attractive. Too butch for me, too bearish. I usually go for tall, lanky guys like myself, with buzzed hair or shaved heads covered in tattoos, piercings all over the place. Mojo has the tattoos, all right—he's been in the business since graduating high school all those years ago, and his arms and legs are covered with ink. He has a few piercings, too, but nothing too outlandish—a few rings in his ears, one in his eyebrow, a stud in the center of his lower lip. But he's a little hairy for me, and bulky…nothing I'd ever thought I'd fall for before I met him.

Now he's all I think about, the guy I compare everyone else to, my ideal lover.

Why the hell does he have to be straight?

"Damn," he says softly. "If I wasn't with Darcy…"

"You'd what?" I want to know. "Admit it, you'd hook up with me?"

Mojo throws me an exasperated glance—he thinks I'm only kidding with him about us getting together, but the truth is, I'd do it if he asked. Hell, who wouldn't?

Only half-teasing, I tell him, "So try telling me you weren't digging my latest ink in the hopes I'd sleep with you. Say it enough times and you just might start to believe it."

"You're the best artist here," he admits. "Besides me."

Despite the pride swelling my chest, I scoff as I clean up my booth. "Here it comes. What do you want?"

Mojo climbs up onto the tattooist chair in front of me and fixes me with a cavalier smile. I know he's working himself up to ask me something he thinks I won't like, so he's turning on the charm. He doesn't have to try too hard to get me interested. "How'd you like to earn some extra cash this weekend?" he asks.

As I'm putting away my ink bottles, I glance at him from the corner of my eye. He's sprawled in the chair, one leg thrown over the armrest so I get a good look at the bulge in his crotch. A big guy like him must have a big-ass dick, or so I've always thought. I'd love to find out.

With the tip of his toe, he nudges my leg. "Come on, say yes."

"I've told you before," I remind him, hedging for time to think things through, "the first time's free. With Darcy knocked up, I know you're hurting for a little something something. I'll let you sample the wares and then we can work out the price."

"What? You're crazy, man." Mojo grins and kicks me playfully, which isn't exactly no, is it? "I'm not renting you out for the weekend, no way. I don't have to *pay* for sex."

I give him a saucy wink. "One taste and you'd want me 24/7. You'd go broke if I charged you *each* time."

Mojo rolls his eyes. "You wish. If Darcy heard you talking like this, she'd—"

"What?" I interrupt. "Want to watch?"

Darcy's in her late twenties, with dyed black hair, colorful tattoos on most of her body, and a fetish for microdermal anchor piercings. Whenever she wants more work done, she works as a receptionist at the 804, scheduling appointments and handling customers in exchange for free tats or anchors. Mojo's been dating her for years, but to hear him tell it, in June the condom finally broke. Three months later, Darcy's usually too nauseous to come into the parlor for long. The last time I saw her, she was starting to show—she wore a cropped concert T-shirt to show off the baby bump and cornered me under the pretense of asking if the tattoos around her navel would stretch out of shape. Before I could give her my opinion, she lowered her voice and pinned me with her fierce, crystal blue eyes. "I'm counting on you to keep Moe in line while I'm knocked up," she said. "If any woman comes in here with designs on my man, you tell me."

With an awkward laugh, I asked, "What about *my* designs on him?"

I don't know if she knows how I feel about Mojo or not, but if she pressed, I would've played it off as a joke, nothing more. Since I started at the parlor, Mojo gets all his tattoos done by me. So technically, my designs *are* on him. In more ways than one.

But the way Darcy smiled at me said she knew exactly what I meant. "I don't want him fooling around with any other *girl*, simple as that."

Was she giving me permission to move in on him? I didn't know at the time and still don't. I don't *think* so, and because Mojo's never done more than parry my advances, I haven't bothered to find out.

Now Mojo leans forward in the chair, the leather creaking under his weight. "Listen to me," he says, as if maybe I haven't been paying attention all this time. "All kidding aside. I got asked to ink at a convention in DC this weekend and said yes."

I frown as I think about what I have planned. *Oh, right, nothing.* "I didn't know there was a show in DC."

Mojo waves my words away with his hand. "It isn't a show. It's some sort of fan con, I don't really understand exactly what for. It runs Friday through Sunday, and the woman in charge of the dealers found me online. She wants a tattoo artist set up for the weekend. The hotel room is comped. Dinner each night, continental breakfast in the morning, lunch on our own."

It sounds too good to be true. I'd been to a few conventions in my youth, mostly comic book cons or sci-fi geek-fests. They're a bit more mellow than a tattoo show, which always has a ton of artists jammed into a large ballroom at some hotel, hawking their designs and haggling with customers to give them the best—and *cheapest*—price on custom ink. "You're the only artist who's going to be there?" I ask, just to be sure.

"Me, myself, and I," Mojo brags. Then he claps a hand on my shoulder and leaves it there, the heat from his touch searing through my thin T-shirt. "And you, if you're in."

Now it's *definitely* too good to be true. The two of us sharing a tiny hotel room for the weekend, working side by side throughout the day and lying inches apart at night...I have to shift on my stool to alleviate the sudden pressure on my balls as my cock stiffens at the thought. "What's it going to cost me?"

"Nothing!" Mojo rocks back in the chair, which squeals in protest. "That's the best part. The lady said she'd comp our room and feed us two meals a day, and even waive the dealer's table fee. She wants a good, quick artist at the con, and hell, you're better than me. With two of us going, we'll earn twice as much money. We set the prices we want to charge, we collect cash, we make out like bandits. It's a bit more intense than working here for three days from noon to eight but it'll definitely be worth it, don't you think?"

I hesitate. Yes, it *will* be intense, hands and arms cramping after three days of nonstop tattooing. *With Mojo*, I remind myself. *Don't forget he'll be there, just the two of you alone in a strange hotel...*

"What about Darcy?" I ask. "Is she going?"

Mojo shakes his head and makes a funny face that tells me she'd never consent to go. "Please. She hates cons. Hell, with the baby on the way, she hates just about everything lately. Last night when I laid down beside her in bed, she told me to stop touching her. What the fuck, you know? It's *my* bed, too. I can't help if it's a bit...*cozy* at times."

Grinning, I ask, "You told her what the fuck?"

"Shit, no." Mojo looks at me like I'm crazy. "I slept on the damn couch. Much more of this and I'm going to crash at your place until the baby's born."

"My bed's big enough for two," I say. "Though I doubt we'd get very much sleep..."

Mojo kicks at me but I scoot out of reach. "We're getting separate beds in the hotel room," he promises. "So, are you in?"

This is Mojo...how can I tell him no?

❖

HE WANTS TO leave Thursday night to avoid rush-hour traffic on the interstate the next morning, since the convention starts early on Friday. So I shove a handful of clothes into a backpack—we're only going to be there a few days—and fill two rolling crates with my tattoo supplies. I take flash art for those customers who'll want a generic design, a pad of carbon paper for those who'll want something I draw up, every bottle of ink I can find, a whole stack of autoclaved needles, an unopened box of latex gloves, surgical soap, A & D ointment, plastic wrap, masking tape, paper towels, witch hazel...everything I think I might possibly need to create art away from my booth.

Mojo has just as much as me, maybe more. He brings along a laptop and printer/scanner combo for anyone who might want to print images off the internet for their tattoos. Somehow he even manages to sneak one of the poseable tattooist chairs out of the 804 on his lunch break, stowing it under a tarp in the back of his pickup. I reschedule the two clients I have down for appointments on Friday and I'm ready to go. The last thing I pack up before I leave work Thursday night is my tattoo machine.

With all our stuff tied down alongside the chair under the tarp, I climb into the pickup's cab and we're off. Mojo swings by a McDonald's to grab a bite to eat before we hit the interstate, and as he's digging out his wallet to pay, he mutters, "Shit."

"What?" I ask, reaching for the wad of twenties crammed into the front pocket of my jeans. "I can get it if you want."

Mojo waves away the offer. "Nah, man, my treat. But I packed my cell into my bag. If Darcy tries to call me, she's going to be pissed when I don't pick up."

I laugh as I take the bag of hamburgers and fries from him.

"What's she going to think? That you're fooling around on her?"

"She knows I'm with you." Mojo reaches into the bag for a handful of fries and I'm all too aware of how close his fingers are to my crotch. Only my jeans and few burgers separate us. "The worst she'll think is we ran off the road and lie bleeding to death in the middle of nowhere."

"That's a happy thought." I shift in my seat, uncomfortable. His hand's still digging in the bag, and the movements are doing wicked things to my budding erection. "What are you looking for in there? Dig any deeper and you're going to be in my pants."

"You'd like that, wouldn't you?" Mojo finally extracts his hand, one of the hamburgers in his grip.

"Damn right," I admit. I take another one of the burgers and unwrap it. The scent of greasy, grilled meat is tantalizing. "Darcy told me I had to keep the girls off you. She never said anything about *me* staying away."

Silence fills the cab as Mojo navigates the Richmond streets, heading for the interstate. For a moment I wonder if I went too far—that was a pretty direct comment, even for me. But the longer I keep quiet, the harder it is to think up a way to apologize. If I said I was sorry and Mojo asked what for, I'd have to explain it…and if he didn't get it in the first place, I don't really want to spell it out. I finish one burger and start on another, wondering if we're going to drive the whole way without saying a word. Then I realize this is *Mojo*, and I don't think the guy's ever been quiet for more than five minutes at a time, let alone two whole hours. He'd die.

Sure enough, as soon as we merge with traffic on the northbound lanes of I-95, Mojo exhales and settles back to finish his burger. "You know the real reason why I asked you to come along this weekend?"

Relief crashes through me like a tidal wave. "I'm thinking it has something to do with my dashing good looks," I joke, glad he brushed off my previous comment the same way he always has.

Mojo answers, "I've been thinking about getting a new tattoo."

To anyone else, this might sound like the start of a whole different conversation. But I hear what Mojo is saying between his words—he likes my work, and wants me along not just to help out at the convention but to give *him* a tattoo at some point over the weekend. "Sounds good," I say, munching on some fries. "What are you thinking about?"

"Just something witty," Mojo says. "I like the letters you did for Darcy's *carpe diem* tat. Back in May, remember?"

I remember. I hate to break it to him, but I have to. "You know that was a font, right? I didn't freehand them."

"I'm not saying I want them specifically," Mojo clarifies. "I'm saying I *like* them, that's all. You do good letter work. I want something short and sweet and I think you can do it."

"I'm sure I can do it, whatever you have in mind." I give him a leer he misses because he's busy watching the road. "Why can't you do it yourself? Everyone knows your letters rock."

Mojo glances in his sideview mirror, studiously avoiding my gaze. He rubs the back of his hand across his mouth, fidgets a little in his seat…is he embarrassed? By what? There's nothing to be embarrassed about if he wants a tattoo in a place he can't reach or see himself. "Moe?" I ask. "I'm not saying I can't do it, man. I will, you know it, anything you'd like. It's cool. Are you thinking maybe across your back or something?"

He gives me a quick look, just a shift of the eyes without moving his head, then grins boyishly. God, he has a sexy smile, slightly crooked, like he's been caught doing something bad but he knows he's going to be able to talk his way out of it easily enough. "I want something to surprise Darcy the next time we do it. *If* we ever do it again. She's a royal bitch now that she's pregnant."

I almost choke on my drink. "Wait, you want me to ink your dick? Ouch!"

"Just above it," he explains. His hand drifts to his lap, where he draws an imaginary curve across his lower belly. "Right here. *Open wide*, maybe, or *say ahh*. I haven't decided yet."

"There are less letters in *say ahh*," I point out. "It'll be quicker. I'm not saying less painful, because you know it's going to hurt like a mother."

Mojo nods. "I know. I've been thinking about it for a while now. I want to do it. I want *you* to do it."

A sly grin spreads across my face. "I get to see your dick," I sing in a childish voice.

With a laugh, Mojo says, "See? There's something in it for you, too."

IT'S LATE BY the time we reach the hotel, and the only room they have available for us has a single kingsize bed. "Great," I mutter as I help Mojo unload our bags and crates onto one of the hotel's luggage carts. "Did you even *ask* if they had any double rooms open?"

"It's fucking eleven o'clock at night," Mojo points out. "Everyone who's coming to this con is already here. We showed up last so we got what was left. Don't sweat it."

Easy for him to say—he isn't going to be trying to sleep with a raging hard-on mere inches from a guy he's been jonesing over months now. As he finishes putting the last of his tattoo supplies onto the cart, he says, "A king size bed is huge, man. It's like as wide as it is long. We can sleep on separate sides and it'll be like we're each in our own bed. You'll see."

"Just wait until we wake up spooned together," I threaten. "When you feel my dick against your ass, you'll *wish* we had separate beds."

"It's a suite," Mojo says, trying to reason with me. "If push comes to shove, I'll sleep on the couch. Heaven knows I'm used to it now with Darcy."

Our room's on the seventh floor. Why we have to truck all our supplies up there instead of leaving them in the dealer's room on third is beyond me, but Mojo says he doesn't want to worry about unpacking everything tonight. "It's late and I'm sure registration is already closed. We'll just set up bright and early in the morning."

"I don't do bright and early," I remind him. "The 804 opens at noon and most days I still can't make it to work on time."

Mojo tosses our backpacks onto the bed and rolls the cart against one wall, our tattoo supplies still boxed up and ready to go. "I don't even know if that floor is secure or not. The last thing I want is to lose a thousand dollars' worth of supplies because I left them in an unlocked dealer's room overnight."

Despite being a suite, our room's a bit on the small side. When we first walk in, there's the bathroom, closet, fridge, even a little mini microwave in case we want to heat anything up. Then there's a den-like area, complete with a wraparound sectional sofa, armchair, desk, and large, flat screen TV. There's another television, same size, in the bedroom area, practically at the foot of the supersized king bed. I sink onto the edge of the mattress and lie back, arms out. Mojo's right—we could probably fit *three* people on this thing and not even realize we weren't sleeping alone.

To prove his point, Mojo flops onto the other side of the bed and stretches out alongside me. Propping his head up on his elbow, he grins down and says, "See? What'd I tell you?"

"You should get one of these for yourself," I joke. "Then Darcy won't be able to complain about you breathing down her neck."

"Her and her damn belly take up our whole bed." Mojo rolls his eyes and sighs. "Some days I can't even begin to imagine why we're doing this, you know? I'm nobody's father."

With a shrug, I admit, "Not yet. You still have a few months to go. Then you're going to be one whether you want to or not."

Mojo picks at the worsted coverlet beneath us. "You ever think about having kids?"

"Oh, no," I say, shaking my head emphatically. "Not me. They're great, don't get me wrong, but that's totally not my thing."

Now Mojo looks at me, a crease furrowing his brows. "Is it because you like guys? I mean, you can always adopt, right?"

"It's because I'm selfish." I sit up and smooth down my T-shirt, suddenly uncomfortable. "Even if I was straight, I wouldn't want kids. I got my art, man. I tattoo and draw and sometimes I get a little dick on the side. I'm not ready to settle down or focus all my attention on someone who isn't me. I got things to do, you know? I got plans, and they don't include kids or a husband, nothing like that. Hell, I can't even commit to a *pet*. No *way* am I going to settle down with children."

Mojo turns to leer at me. "Speaking of a little dick…"

I give him what I hope is a withering look. "If you mean yours, I seriously doubt it's *little* by any stretch of the imagination."

"Let's do the tattoo now," he says, rolling onto his stomach to stare at me. "It's still fairly early. After we set up downstairs tomorrow, we'll probably be there for the rest of the weekend, day and night, inking until our hands fall off. What do you say?"

What *can* I say? He has a point. My jeans tighten around my crotch just thinking about touching him *there*. "You're absolutely sure you want to do this?" I ask. "It's going to hurt like a bitch."

He waves that away. "I have Darcy's name on the inside of my lip, see?" He pulls down his lower lip and shows me. "*That* was a bitch. I think I can handle this."

It takes me a few minutes to dig out my supplies. He wants just black ink, which tells me he *knows* it's going to hurt and he doesn't want to prolong the agony any more than he has to. He settles for *say ahh*, so after I have my machine ready and my needles lined up, I sketch out the letters and try not to watch him undress. Still, I can't help but look—from the corner of my eye, I see him unzip his jeans and slide them down. He's by the foot of the bed, so I can see him perfectly from where I sit on the sofa. He wears a pair of thin boxers under the jeans, and from the way the front bulges a bit, I know he's freeballing underneath.

*God.*

My hand shakes a little and I ball up the piece of paper.

Tossing it aside, I try again. The next time I look up, Mojo stands in front of me with his T-shirt pulled up over his large belly, his boxers hanging low on his hips. With his hand, he draws an imaginary line across his pubic mound—when he does, he tugs at the fabric of his boxers and for one breathless moment, the fly gapes open. "I'm thinking right about here, Can you curve it a bit? Like this?"

My gaze is glued to the front of his boxers. They tent slightly, but I don't know if this is turning him on or if he just got hard when he took off the jeans. "Wray?" he prompts. He draws that line again and I stare into the shadowy gap in his fly, wishing I could make out his cock and balls in the darkness. "Can you curve it?"

"Sure."

My fingers feel nerveless, but the artistic side of my brain takes control. I sketch out the letters without thinking about it, curving them slightly so they'll ride above Mojo's dick like a banner. *Say ahh.* My mind skips ahead—he's a hairy man, will one razor be enough to shave the area clean? Where am I going to put my other hand while I'm working? I'll need to hold him steady while I'm inking him but Jesus, I'll be shaking like a leaf the whole time. Can I do this?

I mean, seriously...*can* I?

*Fuck that,* I tell myself, finishing up the sketch. *You will do it, you will, you have to. If you don't, you'll regret it. Just get into the zone— this is your job. It doesn't matter if it's Mojo or Joe Blow off the street. It's your job.*

He sinks down beside me on the sofa and watches as I finish the letters. Suddenly I'm all too aware of how close he is to me, his chest pressing lightly against my arm, his hand resting so damn close to my leg, it's unnerving. "That's perfect," he breathes. "Who needs a computer when you can hand draw lettering like that? You're good, man. Real good."

The praise warms me up inside. I half-turn, holding the piece of paper between us as if it's going to be much of a buffer. "Let me see where you want it to go."

Mojo leans back on the sofa and pulls up his shirt. I watch him unsnap the front of his boxers—not all the way, just enough to expose the tender skin above the root of his dick. As he works his way down and each snap opens his fly wider, I hold my breath…surely the next snap will show me tawny, tufted hair, kinked at the base of his shaft. I can see the length's shadowy form through the boxers; the fabric is taut above it, and with each snap that opens, it jiggles a bit like a mast slowly rising inch by inch…

But there's no hair.

"I didn't peg you as a manscaper," I tease, daring to stroke the area. I can tell he doesn't shave it normally—I feel slightly raised bumps, *razor burn*. The skin feels hot to my touch, as if Mojo's burning up inside. *For me*, I think, but I'm just flattering myself.

Or am I? When my wrist accidentally bumps against the cock straining his boxers, Mojo gasps and catches his lower lip between his teeth.

Now *that's* a sexy look on him.

Hoping to return to a professional air between us, I hold the piece of paper up to the exposed flesh on his lower abdomen. I try my best to ignore *where* the letters are going and concentrate on the drawing itself. "I'm going to have to go over the spot again with a clean razor," I say, just to fill the silence between us. "You're such a hairy beast, I'm surprised this patch of pubes didn't grow back overnight."

By now there's no denying it—his cock is hard, and the way he looks away from me whenever I glance up at his face tells me he's hoping I don't notice. Hello? How can I not? The thing's practically poking me in the eye, and when I finally start inking down there, I'm going to have to maneuver around it the best I can. It's like an elephant in the room, an embarrassment neither of us wants to mention.

Well, *he* probably doesn't want to mention it, but damn, I want to take a few moments to concentrate on nothing else.

"What's this?" I take the plunge and grab his dick through

his shorts. It feels like sheathed steel in my grip; I give it a little squeeze and feel it stiffen in my fist. God, he's huge.

I expect him to slap my hand away—get angry, yell, something. Instead he surprises me by laying his head back against the sofa and moaning my name. "Wray, Jesus. Took you long enough. I thought I was going to bust a nut before you noticed."

I stroke his length through his boxers. "Wait, you *want* me to do this?"

He moans again and nods, his whole body relaxing. His legs spread farther apart, easing him down into the cushions a little, and the boxers gap open less than an inch above where my hand holds his dick. "You always talk a good game," Mojo says, one hand rubbing over his stomach as I knead his shaft between my fingers. "Don't tell me you're having second thoughts now."

"You're straight," I remind him. When I start to pull my hand away, he clasps both of his over my wrist, holding it in place. "What about Darcy?"

Through half-closed lids, Mojo gives me a sardonic look. "She already thinks we're doing it. We might as well—"

"And she's cool with it?" I ask, incredulous. *Thanks for telling me sooner. Shit.*

"She always says she'd crack my balls if I screw around on her with another woman," Mojo explains. "But she doesn't want me touching *her*, so finally I was like, then what the hell am I supposed to do, you know? And she goes, what, isn't Wray putting out?"

I laugh as I spread my fingers across the bulge in the front of Mojo's boxers. His grip relaxes when he realizes I'm not going to stop what I'm doing—actually, now that I have Darcy's blessing, I don't *want* to stop. My skin tingles where it brushes along Mojo's shaved flesh, then I dip my fingertips down into the fly of Mojo's boxers and pop open the remaining buttons.

His heavy dick swings up to meet me. It's thick and veined, the cockhead a ruddy brown that reminds me of autumn leaves. A trickle of clear liquid bubbles from the tip, tracing down the slit on the underside. The way it curves up to meet me says Mojo's just as eager as I am to take this moment between us and stretch it out into the night, as far as it will go. He's a good seven inches hard, easily two inches wide—I was right, he's got a fat cock, and I want it, from root to tip. I want it all.

But I hesitate. We have a great thing between us, an easygoing relationship, a bromance unlike anything I have with anyone else in my life. Part of the reason for that is because I've always felt safe in the illusion that, no matter how much I teased and flirted, he stayed just beyond my reach. He was straight, untouchable, not mine. Anything we do from here on out, anything at all, changes everything.

With the tip of my forefinger, I trace down along the underside of his dick. I watch the way it responds to my touch—how it quivers, eager for more. "If we do this," I start, raising my gaze to meet Mojo's.

He stares at me with an open expression I never thought I'd see in his eyes. "Wray, I'm not into guys. I'm just not. I love Darcy, you know. But we have something, man. Something here— " He clenches his T-shirt in a fist and taps the middle of his chest, indicating his heart. "I…I think I love you, too."

The admission should send me running for the hills—I'm not the type to fall in love, I'm *not*. But I know what he means—there *is* something, call it love, call it lust, call it curiosity or whatever you want, it's a tie binding us together. If we *do* this, the knot will only tighten. We'll be pulled together, closer than before.

And Darcy's cool with it, and Mojo's offering me a chance I never thought I'd get. Why would I possibly turn it down?

I don't know what to say. I'm not a romantic; the word 'love' doesn't come easy for me, even to family. My mother came to terms with this years ago. I've never said it to another man and, no matter how awesome I think Mojo is, he isn't going to be the first to hear it from me. His admission hangs between us awkwardly, like a grenade with a pulled pin, waiting to explode. We're both waiting—I'm half as hard as he is, and the fact he's bared himself to me, body and soul, spurs on the erection growing in my jeans. I need to say something, do something, anything, before the moment slips away from me and is gone.

So I do the only thing I can think to do—I take it firmly in hand, take *Mojo* in hand, clasp my fingers tight around his thick cock even as I unzip my jeans. I lean toward him, my grip fast around the root of his dick, and begin to massage his shaft with a rhythmic pumping of my fist. My other hand flays open my fly and pulls my briefs down below my balls, pushing my cock out like an exclamation pointing from my jeans.

Mojo stares at me, breathless. His gaze shifts from my dick to my face and back again, and when he licks the corner of his mouth, I know this is it, this is real, it's happening. He wants me, even if he doesn't yet know why or how.

There's a half-empty tube of A & D ointment resting among the supplies I set out for Mojo's tattoo. Without releasing my hold on his dick, I reach over and snag the tube, tossing it his way. He fumbles with it but doesn't drop it. "Put some in your hand," I tell him.

He obeys. The clear gelatinous blob quivers in his palm a moment, then he closes his fingers over it to squish it flat. Taking his wrist, I guide him to my crotch. His fingers tighten, almost as if they're afraid to open, but when I bump his knuckles against my stiff dick, he relaxes and his fingers open like the petals of a flower. "What am I supposed to do?" he asks, daring to brush my length with his fingertips.

"Just jerk me off," I say. I give his own cock an encouraging squeeze as if to show him how. "My dick works the same way as yours."

For a moment longer, his hand hovers near my dick. I'm aching for him—just take it, *please*—and I'm just about to tell him he's not getting off if *I* don't when his fingers encircle my length. The ointment squelches against my skin, then lubricates his hand as he begins to slide it up and down. Waves of pleasure crash over me. "Yeah," I tell him, nodding as my own hand finds a similar rhythm on his dick. "Just like that."

"Do you need the tube?" he asks. His voice is hushed, as if he can't believe he's doing this.

But I have other plans—I shake my head and, as he watches, lean down to kiss the tip of his dick.

"God, Wray," Mojo sighs. His hand freezes on my cock in mid-stroke. "Oh, God, you're not...I mean, you—"

"I'm going to suck your dick," I say. The way he trembles all over tells me this might be the first blowjob he's ever had. "Don't tell me Darcy doesn't do this."

He can't speak, but he shakes his head a little in disbelief. "She's never...I mean, she doesn't..." He licks his lips and squeezes my cock so hard, I almost come right there. "Do it again. Can you? Can you do it again?"

Staring into his eyes, I watch him watch me as I lean down again. I pucker just to prolong the inevitable, and I have to admit I like the way he catches his breath as I move in. When my lips touch the tender head of his cock, he bites his lower lip and moans unconsciously. Without pulling back, I run my tongue over my lips and at the same time over his glans because it's so close. He gasps, his gaze glued to my mouth as if he doesn't want to miss whatever it is I plan to do next.

After rimming the flared tip, I lap at the slit on the underside, then close my lips around the plum-like head.

Pain sears through my groin. I reach for my cock, caught in Mojo's death grip, and rub his wrist to relax his hand. "Easy, man," I say, sitting back. "If you're going to strangle it, I'm going to have to stop."

"Sorry." With a sheepish grin, he lets me guide his hand up and down again, slowly, finding a steady pace. "Like this?"

I nod. "Better. Just don't stop, okay? Just—ah, yes, *that*. That works."

He rubs his thumb along the bottom of my dick, up my slit and down again, up all the way to cover the tip and down to the base where my balls begin. Long, even strokes, comforting, mesmerizing. If the pace never picked up, I could stay here in this state of semi-arousal for the rest of my life.

But I want more than this, and I know Mojo does, too. Leaning into his crotch again, I lick down the length of his shaft to his balls and press my mouth into the gaping fly of his boxers. Now I can feel kinked hair tickle my lips and chin—his balls are nestled in a fine fuzz that smells of sex and musk. I stick my tongue down in there and taste Mojo's unique flavor, manly and sweaty and a little ripe. It's the same taste I get from the pre-cum glistening at the tip of his dick, and it spurs me on. I want more.

I go down again, taking his full length between my lips. His cock fills my mouth, rubbing against the roof of it, then tickling the back of my throat. My hand flattens his balls down into the darkness of his boxers and I gently pinch my forefinger and thumb together, massaging him in time with his strokes on my erection. On my way up, I swirl my tongue along his length, licking it as I would a lollipop, savoring his scent and his flavor, the man, the moment, *this. Us.*

I cover his cockhead with little prickling kisses, then trail them down his shaft, kissing away the beads of my own saliva slicking his dick. At the base, I open wide and, covering my teeth with my lips, press my mouth around him, sticking my tongue out as if I could possibly encircle him with it. I raise my head, sliding my mouth up his length; at the top, I cover his knob with my mouth and release it, my head on the other side of his dick now, trailing back down the other side.

He moans above me. "Jesus, Wray. That's so fucking hot."

With a subtle thrust of my hips, I remind him to keep his hand moving on my dick. Then I go down on him again—I'm through playing. Closing my lips over his cockhead, I begin to rub his slit with my tongue as I suck in my cheeks. He seems to swell in my mouth, and I get the first teasing taste of the bittersweet saltiness of his seed. I go down on him once, twice, then concentrate on his tip again, suckling it, trying to draw him towards release.

From the faint mewling sound he makes, I know I'm succeeding.

Keeping the tip of his dick behind my front teeth, I stretch my tongue down his length as far as it will go. I'm no Gene Simmons, but I've never developed much of a gag reflex, so I can reach pretty far. His dick buts against my palette as I dive farther, my tongue angling to taste his balls. Mojo fucks up into me, forcing his cock deep into my throat, and I swallow to constrict the muscles around his erection.

"Yes," he sobs, jerking me off with one meaty fist. He's close to coming—I can feel the tension in his dick, the subtle tightening of the skin that always tells me a guy's going to shoot his load, and he's yanking on my dick as if he's trying to pull it out by the root. "God, yes, *yes*."

One more long pull does it. His ass rises off the sofa as he ejaculates. Hot jism fills the back of my throat as I drink him down. The taste and scent of his orgasm triggers my own release—my cock spurts onto his fingers, slicking them with my juices. "Jesus," he sighs. "Just…oh God, that was good."

I pull my head back, letting him slip from my throat into my mouth. Tenderly I nibble on his bulbous tip one last time before releasing it. "You've got a fat one on you," I say, wiping my mouth with the back of my hand. "And you come too damn quick."

His grin slowly dissolves. "It was my first time."

"I know. We'll have to work on that." I reach for the hand still gripping my dick and, peeling the fingers off me one by one, I lace mine between them. Semen and A & D ointment squish between us.

A slow smile crosses Mojo's face. "So you're saying you're cool with this?"

I don't *say* anything—my response is a smoldering look that brings a faint flush to his cheeks. Locking my gaze with his, I raise our hands to my lips and stick out my tongue. As he watches me, I lick my cum off his knuckles, one by one. By the time I'm finished, his mouth is slack, his eyes hooded with lust. Between us, his cock has begun to stand up and take notice again.

❖

THE TATTOO ITSELF only takes an hour—I'm usually quick with letters, but Mojo's skin above his pubic area is delicate and thin, so I'm more careful than usual to make sure the lines are crisp and tight. He wiggled a bit when I was putting on the transfer, and I had to get him to hold his dick to one side, out of the way, so it would stop bumping against my wrist, but other than gritted teeth and a grimace as I worked, he weathered it fine.

It isn't until I'm taping a sheet of clear plastic wrap over the area that I realize what he said earlier about Darcy. "Hold up," I say, pausing with my hand over his lower belly.

"What?" he sighs. His face is still flushed and he's sweating a little, but whether it's because of the endorphins flooding his system after the tattoo or the erection held tight in his hand, I don't know.

Smoothing the wrap flat over his new ink, I look at the words and the angry skin around them. "You said you wanted to surprise Darcy with this."

He grins wickedly. "She has no clue I asked you to do this. When she sees it, she's going to flip."

"But then you said she's never gone down on you," I point out. "So why bother?"

He looks down at the tattoo. "*I'll* know it's there. Hell, by the time she lets me touch her again, the hair will have all grown back anyway and you'll need a weed whacker to get to it."

Then he covers my hand with his, pressing my palm flat against his lower belly. The skin feels hot beneath my touch. "And *you'll* know it's there," he says, slipping his fingers under mine. "Think of it as an open invite."

I laugh as I start to put away my tattooing supplies. "So now it's like that between us, is it?"

Mojo's smile slips a little. "Like what?" When I shake my head but don't answer, he catches my wrist and forces me to look at him. "Wray, I thought you were cool with this. With…with us."

"Let me ask you this." I stop what I'm doing and face him squarely—I want to watch him answer me, to make sure I get this straight…or rather, as straight as it could ever possibly be between two men. "Look at me, Mojo, so I'll know if you're lying or not."

"I'm not—"

"Let me get the question out first."

His mouth snaps shut.

Taking a deep breath, I ask him, "Is this just something you want to do while Darcy's not putting out for you? Once the baby's here, are things going to go back to the way they were— the blue-ball flirting without either of us putting out for the other?"

Mojo frowns and shakes his head. "Wray, no…"

"Or is this something you want to follow through on?" I ask, speaking over him. "Not just me getting you off but something mutual, something more? Because if it's just going to be me blowing you now and then, we can go back to being friends and forget tonight ever happened."

"No." Mojo shakes his head again, emphatic. "Wray, listen. I want you, I do. Darcy knows it…hell, she knew it before I did myself. And she's okay with it, really. She knows there are things one guy can do for another that a woman can't."

"She can lick your dick as well as I can," I say, unconvinced. "Probably better. She has that tongue piercing—"

"Wray." Taking both my hands in his, Mojo pulls me to him. I have to be mindful of the fresh ink on his belly, so I let him pull me up off the coffee table where I gave him the tattoo and then sit perched on his knees. When he looks at me, the expression in his eyes is everything I've always wanted to see shining back. "This is all new to me, but I want it. I want *you*. And I know you've wanted me for so damn long now. So can't you give me a chance? Let me prove there's something deeper than friendship between us. Show me what to do and I'll do it. Show me how to love you, and I will."

There's that word again, *love*. If he says it enough times, I might let myself start to believe it.

Sliding down his thighs, I sit in his lap and lean forward until my forehead touches his. This close, his eyes are mesmerizing. "I can't really *show* you how to do it," I murmur, my words soft in the intimate space between us. "Just think about whatever it is you'd want to have done to you, and do it to me instead."

Mojo wraps his arms around my waist. "How will I know if I'm doing it right?"

I touch my mouth to his in a sweet kiss—the first of many. "We'll have to keep practicing until you get it."

I feel his lips smile against mine. "If we're lucky, this could take all night."

I've never felt luckier.

# The Tattooed Heart

WHEN LEE ENTERS Tattoo 804, Chris is just finishing up with a client. Though it's less than thirty minutes to closing time, April's behind the counter and knows Lee's a friend, so she waves him back to Chris's booth. "Hey, man," Chris says, glancing up from the ornate Celtic knot armband he's been coloring in for a while now. The client, a pretty woman in her late twenties, grins at Lee with gritted teeth. Chris motions to a nearby chair. "Have a seat. I'm almost through."

Lee's two years older than Chris but they go way back. The first day after winter break when Chris had been in the fourth grade, to be exact; Lee had been a burly sixth grader, scary as shit, patrolling the playground at their elementary school with the other tough boys in his class. Chris, always on the small side, often fell prey to the bullies. When Lee came over to pick on him that cold January afternoon, Chris was sitting on the frozen ground, one pant leg pulled up to expose an intricate pattern he'd been drawing on himself with a ballpoint pen. He expected to be laughed at, jeered, maybe even punched if he couldn't dodge fast enough. The last thing he'd been ready for was to find the older boy hunkering down beside him as Lee pulled up the leg of his own jeans. "Great tat. Think you can do one on me?"

Funny how life turns out. At thirty, Chris rents a booth at Tattoo 804, an up-and-coming tattoo parlor in Richmond located less than a mile from the schoolyard where he first met Lee. Most of his clients aren't looking for anything custom, not yet—they want hearts on their wrists or paw prints on their ankles, or someone's name scribbled somewhere on their bodies. His own art is hidden away in portfolios he never shows anyone but Lee. They've been friends forever, and when Chris has a new design he'd like to etch into someone, who else would he call?

Lee sinks onto a stool near the mirror by Chris's booth. He leans down to look at the armband, careful to stay out of the light. "That's tight, man. Real sharp. You oughta do one for me."

"I got plans for you," Chris promises. He wipes away excess ink and a trace amount of blood, studies his handiwork, then dives back in.

From the corner of his eye, he sees Lee in the mirror—it's June and already hot out, so Lee wears one of those faded tank tops called a wifebeater that shows off the ink on his arms. Chris did every single tattoo on Lee's body, each a custom design, a tribute to his art. He's not the only one looking; the woman in his chair turns her head and checks Lee out. Dark, mussed hair that looks like he just got out of bed. Warm eyes that crinkle into half-moons when he laughs. Heart-shaped lips most women would kill to have. They'd look girly if he wasn't so damn built. Lee works construction, and Chris is never sure if he wears those dirty jeans and clunky boots for looks or function. Noticing his newest tattoo, a colorful maze Chris did a month ago spiraled around Lee's left elbow, the woman says, "Nice tats. Where'd you get them done?"

"Here." Lee gives her a wink that makes her blush. "You're in the hands of the best, babe. Nobody inks me but Chris."

When the armband's finally done, Chris wraps it in cellophane and tells the woman to keep it clean. "I know what to do," she promises, slipping him a neatly folded ten when he helps her out of the chair. "You aren't my first. I really like your touch, and those designs on your friend are killer. I'll definitely be back."

Lee waits until she reaches the front desk before he takes her place in the chair in front of Chris. "What's up?" he asks, watching as Chris cleans his station. "I ain't heard from you in a while. Keeping busy?"

A slow smile spreads across Chris's face. "You could say that. I got a man now, Lee. I have to be home nights."

Lee claps his hands and whoops, a little too loudly. "All *right!*"

Chris ducks his head, embarrassed, but there aren't many people in the parlor this late. "Keep it down," he says, even though he can't stop grinning. "It's not all that."

"Not *yet*," Lee points out. "But you want it to be?"

Chris laughs. "I think so, yeah. I think he's the one."

As he clears away the small cups of ink and water from his table, his mind drifts to Barry. The dude is everything Chris wants in a lover, there's no denying it. Tall, slim, sexy, even if he doesn't have any tattoos yet. That'll change. Chris has offered to ink Barry himself for free and Barry said maybe, yeah. Another couple months and Chris thinks that "maybe, yeah" will turn into "please."

"Where'd you meet him?" Lee's voice is quieter now, subdued. "Is he hot?"

The look Chris gives his friend says it all. "Shyeah. Hot as shit. He plays guitar in April's brother's band and we met after his set one night at the Code downtown. Just hooked up and hit it off. I am officially in love."

When Chris glances at his friend, Lee's grin slides into place, but when he turns, he sees it slip away in the mirror. There's something unsettling about how Lee stares at him, something that says wheels are turning inside that bushy head of his. "I know what you're thinking," Chris says.

That earns him an amused grunt. "What's that?"

"It's too early to tell." Chris laughs and shakes his head. "Man, whatever. He's all into me, that's all I'm saying. Finally, you know? A guy who wants to be with me twenty-four seven, who likes my art, who wants me to draw something special for his first tattoo and put the image on him myself. Where else am I ever gonna find someone like that?"

In the mirror, Lee's heart-shaped mouth twists into a strangled knot. "Hell if I know."

When Chris turns toward him, that sour pucker has smoothed out and he thinks maybe he imagined it. "What 'cha got for me tonight?" Lee asks, clapping his hands together. "Are they cool with you staying late for a client?"

"A client? No." Chris reaches for his portfolio, tucked into the space between his table and the wall. "But man, you're a friend. This ain't a sale. Let me show you what I've been doing. How's your own love life going?"

Lee takes the offered portfolio and flips to the back without being asked, where he knows Chris's newer work is kept. "Pssh," he says, dismissive. "My problem is the guys I like never like me back. These sketches are good. More mazes?"

"They're not really." Chris rolls his stool around so he's beside Lee's chair and leans against his friend's arm as he traces one of his more elaborate drawings. "It's one continuous line, see? They just bend sharply and fold back behind the first line, sort of like that old Windows screensaver, I guess. You know, the one with the pipes? I can leave 'em hollow or color them in, any color you want. I'm thinking they'd look damn cool on your shoulder and flowing over down your arm, you know? I can do as much or as little as you like."

Lee's arm burns through Chris's shirt. "Whatever you want," he murmurs. "It's up to you."

Chris looks up to find his friend staring at him openly and he grins to alleviate the sudden tension between them. "Great!

Let's get started. Take off your shirt for me, will you?"

LEE'S FIRST TATTOO was a black and red star on the back of his right hand. It was the first tattoo Chris ever did, and no matter how much Chris tries to cajole Lee into letting him redo it, Lee won't let him. "It's crap," Chris has said. "I've gotten so much better."

But Lee is adamant. "I like it. Shows just how far you've come. You can touch it up but don't you dare cover it over."

As Chris sets up for Lee's next tattoo, this Möbius strip-like pipe, Lee flips through the portfolio in his hands. Chris is an awesome artist, one of the best. A consummate professional, too, with a light touch and unique designs. The moment they met all those years ago, Lee knew Chris would be doing something with his art later on in life. Lee couldn't draw stick figures, let alone these gorgeous sketches that fill Chris's portfolio. There are dragons and birds, vicious sabertooth cats, sexy women and hulking men, hooded skeletons, Celtic-inspired knots, and everywhere these new pipe things Chris currently favors.

At the bottom of each page, a pair of young boys scamper at the edge, seeming to move when Lee flips the pages. The boys look suspiciously like the two friends did as children—one is small and slim, obviously Chris, the other stocky and tall, like Lee himself. He stops at one image where the boys hunch down beside a short stream. "What's this?"

"Up." Chris motions Lee to stand so he can adjust the chair properly. It needs to lie flat so Lee's back and shoulder will be within easy reach. As it adjusts, he glances at the page Lee holds open and laughs. "Just something I'm playing around with, man. They're kind of cute, aren't they?"

Lee grunts, noncommittal. "They look like—"

"They're Barry and me," Chris tells him, then shrugs. "Or they're supposed to be. I'm still figuring out just what I want them to be doing when I tattoo him. Sit.'"

Without a word, Lee closes the portfolio and sets it aside. He stretches, savoring the pop in his muscles because he isn't sure when he'll get the chance to stretch again. Those two boys dance around his thoughts, but he pushes them aside and climbs onto the now stretched-out chair beside Chris's stool. He lays on his stomach, right arm angled out, left arm curled under his cheek. In the mirror, he watches Chris prepare to get to work.

Those two boys looked like himself and Chris, not this Barry person Chris just met. Doesn't he know Lee would let him put that image anywhere he wanted? The boys could be doing anything, anything at all. Lee's body is Chris's canvas and always has been. Why can't Chris see that?

Lee catches a glimpse of his own troubled reflection and looks away.

Chris works in silence. He sets up the ink he'll use—just black tonight, since he'll just do the outline first—and debates which gauge needle to use. Lee watches him, wondering once again what it is he finds so attractive about his friend. Chris isn't much to look at, to be sure. He's always been a head shorter than Lee and scrappy thin. He has a long, narrow face, bushy black eyebrows, and shoulder-length hair the color of spilled ink. He wears it tucked behind his ears, and while at work he hides it under a baseball cap, so the ends want to curl when they escape. His dark hair and naturally dusky skin frame his pale blue eyes perfectly—they're large, expressive, and more than once, Lee's thought of them in his sleep and woken with a bad erection. Dreamy eyes, Lee might call them, if he let himself think of Chris that way. Soulful eyes. *Damn.*

In addition to his multiple tattoos, Chris has a few piercings, as well. A silver hoop juts from one eyebrow, and a circular barbell hangs from his nasal septum. Lee hasn't gone in for any other body mods himself—Chris doesn't do the piercings, so Lee isn't tempted to let his friend talk him into one. But if Chris did? Lee knows he'd look like a human pin cushion in no time. Whenever Chris calls him up, Lee's already heading for Tattoo 804. He just can't tell Chris no.

After Chris applies the transfer, which sets the tattoo's image onto Lee's skin, he asks, "Do you want to take a look before we get started?"

"Nah, man. I'm cool." Lee grins and gives Chris a wink. "I trust you."

"Ready, then?" Chris wheels his stool up close and runs a hand along the sensitive underside of Lee's arm. Despite the latex gloves he wears, Lee's skin warms at the touch.

Lee nods as Chris settles in. "Go to it."

As the needle buzzes, Lee's mind goes blank. He stares at the mirror, at his own eyes staring back, until he can't stand to look at himself any more and shifts his gaze to watch Chris. His back grows hot where the tattoo takes shape—it always feels like rug burn to him, not painful but not really all that great, either. Still, seeing Chris hovering above him, concentrating so readily on his body, creating something personal and new where before there was nothing but blank skin...a familiar ache settles into Lee's balls. When Chris sits back to shift into a better position, Lee takes a moment to bend one knee, just slightly. Just enough to let up on the pressure at his crotch, where he's already sporting wood. Chris doesn't miss the gesture. "You getting hard?" he teases.

Lee shifts a little on the table to take his weight off his throbbing cock. He can't meet Chris's dancing gaze in the mirror. "You know how I am."

"Man," Chris drawls, turning back to the tattoo. "I wish getting inked turned me on."

Hoping to change the subject, Lee asks, "Who does you?"

Too late, he realizes his question might be misinterpreted— he means which artist tattoos Chris, not who gets his friend hard. He doesn't want to hear about this new guy of Chris's, Barry whatever the hell his name is. Each week Chris seems to find someone new, and the way he goes on and *on* about his latest piece of ass always makes Lee sad. How long has *he* been waiting here for his chance? When will Chris finally tire of everyone else and notice *him*?

Fortunately, Chris knows what he's asking. They've been friends so damn long. "April did my last one," he says, pulling Lee's skin taut so he can continue his design. "Don't move. This is tricky."

"There's your problem," Lee jokes. "A chick isn't going to get your blood pumping, even if she does have an ink gun in one hand and piercings up the wazoo."

Chris snickers; Lee feels his friend's breath cool his heated flesh. "I don't know if she has any piercings *there*."

"God, I don't *want* to know." Lee smiles when Chris laughs, careful not to laugh himself and ruin the tattoo. "All I'm saying is get a hot guy to ink you, then let me know if you get hard."

"Don't let Barry hear you say that," Chris warns. He's only teasing, but his words sting and the smile fades from Lee's face. "He probably wouldn't like knowing my best friend thinks I'm hot."

Lee doubts this Barry ass is smart enough to put two and two together. Hell, Lee's known Chris for going on twenty years now and Chris has never clued in.

BECAUSE OF ITS intricate design and sheer size, the tattoo takes several weeks to complete. The first night, Chris outlines the entire thing, which takes longer than he expected—the tattoo is a writhing mass of sharp angles and long lines starting just above a freckle on the back of Lee's upper arm. It curves up his bicep, around his armpit, following the lines of his body. Around his shoulder it flares out, filling up most of that side of Lee's back, then trickles down to end a few inches below his shoulder blade. The outline itself takes a good two hours of nothing but intense concentration, Chris's hand steady as he grips the tattoo gun, his world nothing but black ink on pale skin and the faint smell of Old Spice deodorant wafting up from Lee as he works. It's a smell Chris has come to associate with late nights at the tattoo parlor, the buzz of the needles, the cool splash of surgical soap against the plastic gloves he wears. It's a smell that slips seductively into his unconsciousness and seizes him by the balls, kneading them like an attentive lover. If getting inked turns Lee on, inking Lee turns *Chris* on. Having someone lie beneath him, patient and still, while he draws his art into their willing flesh…it's a heady rush, he has to admit.

In the quiet parlor, Lee watches Chris in the mirror as he works. Neither speak; neither have to. Chris traces his own outlines carefully, leaning in close to ensure every pore is filled with dark ink just where he wants it. When he finishes a section, he squirts the green soap onto it, wipes away the excess ink and faint traces of blood from his art, then moves onto the next section. And the next. And the next.

Lee heals quickly—he always does. When he comes in at the end of the following week, the tattoo has already finished peeling. Chris redoes the outline, darkening it, then begins to fill in one little corner of the image with a vibrant blue. He thinks maybe he'll color the whole design with this color—it's gorgeous, really, and with Lee looking back over one shoulder to watch Chris work, Chris can see the shade mirrors the same sexy blue of his friend's eyes. He'll fade it, though, and the final touch will be a thin line of paler blue, maybe silvery white, right through the center of the pipe to make it look like it's reflecting the light. When he's done, it'll look fucking awesome.

He only colors in part of the tattoo that second night. Lee comes back a third week, and a fourth, before the whole thing is done. By the end of the month, Chris is back to touching up the first fill work he did so long ago. Solid colors sometimes fall out a bit when healing, and intricate designs such as this take longer to complete. He'll have Lee come back again, maybe one more time, because even though most of the tattoo has healed nicely, Chris doesn't want to spend all night at the parlor. He has plans. Lee must sense his excitement because there's a faint look of amusement dancing in his eyes. "You still seeing that guy?" he asks when Chris sits back to shake the cramps out of his hand.

"Barry? Yeah." Chris grins and knows he's on the verge of gushing. It's been over a month now, and things are going strong between them. "You gotta meet him, man. You two will get along great."

Lee's gaze drifts away and he frowns as he tries to look over his shoulder to see the tattoo taking shape behind him. "You inked him yet?"

With a laugh, Chris leans in to tackle the last bit of touch-up he plans to do tonight. "He's holding out on me. He's worse than a damn virgin afraid of popping his cherry. I tell him it don't hurt but he doesn't believe me." He runs a hand down the curve of Lee's back where a dragon's spine is tattooed—the first large tat Chris did, and it *still* looks killer. "I gotta introduce you two. Then *you* can tell him it doesn't hurt all that much. Hell, it even turns you on."

Playfully, his hand drifts over Lee's taut buttocks to poke at the soft sac hidden between them. Through Lee's jeans, Chris barely feels a thing, but his friend gasps as if goosed. "Don't move!" Chris chides, laughing. He holds the tattoo gun high to avoid touching Lee with it. "I don't want to fuck this up now."

"Don't cop a feel," Lee says. The grin on his lips barely reaches his eyes. "What'd Barry have to say if he saw *that*?"

"Please." Chris holds Lee's arm steady as he finishes with the tattoo. "We've been friends for so long, Lee, you're like a brother to me. I can tease you if I want. Besides, what happens when I run out of room up here and have no where else to ink but your cock and balls? You expect me to do it blindfolded?"

Lee's eyes go wide, but Chris can't interpret the emotion glistening in them. Fear? Excitement? A little bit of both?

"You're not inking my balls," he whispers. "Are you?"

Chris winks at him but doesn't reply. For a long moment the two friends stare at each other, unable to look away, each assessing the other. Then one of them snickers—Chris doesn't know who does it first, him or Lee, but soon they're both snorting with laughter. "You ain't inking my balls," Lee says again. "You ain't *touching* them."

"You never know," is all Chris will commit to at the moment.

Of course, he doesn't mention it to Barry. He doesn't have to—he and Lee were just goofing around. But he *does* talk up the new tattoo to his lover. He can't help it. The design turns out gorgeous, if he says so himself, and it took a good six weeks to finalize. He has every right to be proud of it. The next time Barry comes over to Chris's studio apartment after a long practice set with his band, Chris can't stop bragging. They sit on the futon, which is folded up into a couch at the moment. An empty pizza box rests on the coffee table before them and the TV is on low, tuned to one of the reality shows which have replaced the music videos MTV used to show. "God, babe," Chris sighs, finishing his last slice of pizza. "You gotta see it. It goes from here—" He touches Barry's arm where Lee's tattoo starts, then spreads his hand and walks it along a path over Barry's shoulder to halfway down his back. "All the way down to here. It's fucking amazing. You'd love it."

Barry's jaw works as he chews. "Hmm."

"The colors just pop," Chris continues. He's gushing but he can't help it—he loves talking about tattoos. "I didn't really know how it'd play out at first, you know? Having that blue blend into the white like that, but it really came together in the end. Lee thinks it's wicked cool. He says—"

"Chris, please." Barry turns toward him, a sardonic look in his eyes. He looks haggard and worn out, the day-old scruff on his chin a dark contrast to his pale skin. His dyed black hair frizzes out around his head like a disheveled halo. Eyeliner smudges look like bruises around his dark eyes. Speaking slowly as if afraid Chris won't understand him otherwise, Barry says, "I am exhausted. Physically and mentally. The last thing I want to talk about is your friend Lee. *Capice?*"

With a laugh, Chris tells him, "You two are so much alike. I can't wait for you to meet him. Then you'll get a chance to see my art first-hand instead of just in my portfolio."

"Chris." Barry whines this time and rolls his eyes. "Please. Two minutes without talking about tattoos or your goddamn friend. Is that too much to ask?"

Chris frowns, confused. What'd he say? "You don't want to talk about tattoos?" What *else* is there to talk about?

Barry sighs, defeated. Turning his attention back to the television, he mumbles, "You didn't even ask how my day went."

"You said you'd been practicing—"

"I didn't say *why.*" Another sigh, this one exasperated. Barry bites into his slice of pizza and tears at it viciously.

Chris knows why they were practicing. Hello, it's a band? Isn't that what they did? When Barry came over, the first thing Chris asked was how he's doing. That right there should've been opening enough to tell him anything Barry wanted to share. His response had just been a short grunt. How was Chris supposed to interpret that? They weren't saying anything a moment ago, just sitting here eating, watching TV, and he mentioned Lee's new tattoo in passing. If Barry wants to talk about something else, he can just bring it up. No use playing these stupid games.

But there's an uneasy tension between them and Chris doesn't know if it's his fault or not, so he'll play along for now. "So why?"

For a long moment, Barry doesn't answer. He's sulking a little, Chris knows. To draw him out, Chris trails a hand over Barry's shoulder, a ticklish touch Barry tries to shrug off but can't. Chris lets his fingers explore, smoothing down the ragged threads from Barry's torn sleeve then rubbing over warm skin, counting the freckles that dot Barry's shoulder one by one, following the trail they create which leads to a tender spot behind Barry's earlobe. There Chris runs his forefinger behind Barry's ear, softly, oh so softly, tracing the curve of skin and feeling it warm beneath his touch. Around the top of Barry's ear to the stud pierced into the cartilage. Chris swirls his finger around the stud, turning it clockwise as he leans close to his boyfriend, closer, *closer*, until his mouth is inches from Barry's lobe and his breath heats the space between them. "Tell me why," he purrs in a low voice.

From the way Barry shifts beside him, one hand drifting to adjust the bulge at the front of his jeans, Chris knows just what he's doing to the man. Whatever argument had been brewing minutes ago dissolves beneath Chris's words. "Barry," he sighs, nipping Barry's earlobe between his teeth. "You gonna tell me? Or do I have to guess?"

A hand drifts to Chris's knee, gives it a squeeze, then rubs higher up his thigh, easing under the hem of his shorts to rub along tender flesh. "Tell you what?" Barry asks, dazed.

Chris snickers and fists his hand in the mess of curls atop Barry's head. "About your band, remember? You wanted me to ask about your practice. So I'm asking. Why—"

Suddenly Barry turns toward him, cutting off his question with a forceful kiss. Chris finds himself pressed back against the futon, pinned beneath Barry, whose hands fumble with the zipper on Chris's shorts. Somehow amid hungry kisses they manage to lose the clothing between them, and any further attempts at conversation disappear.

LESS THAN TWO weeks go by before Lee gets another call from Chris. "Swing by the parlor tonight, could you?" his friend asks.

As if he'd say no. "What's up? You got another design in mind so soon?"

When Chris laughs, the sound warms Lee up inside. "Just

come on over around closing time. I'll see you then?"

Of course. If Chris wanted him there now, Lee would drop everything to comply. But he waits until quarter to eight, his whole body humming with nervous energy that chases him around his small townhouse, up and down the stairs, nipping at the edges of his thoughts. Chris and he alone in the parlor after hours, the room dark around them, the only light coming from the small, hot lamp shining down on Chris as he inks another design into Lee's skin. The insane pressure that builds in Lee's groin when his friend is tattooing him—he's never let another artist work on him so he doesn't know if it's the pain that turns him on or if it's really Chris, leaning over him, breath soft against Lee's skin, hands firm and commanding while holding Lee in place.

And the last time they'd been together, when Chris joked about inking Lee's boys? God, if it ever came to that, Lee knows he'll be rock solid hard the whole time. He'll have to sit on his hands to keep from jerking off. He pictures Chris between his legs, leaning in close, tattoo gun in one hand buzzing and the other holding Lee's erect cock up out of the way. Chris's soft breath *there*, his firm touch in places Lee's only dreamed of it...Lee will be lucky if he doesn't shoot a load right in his friend's face before the needles even touch his flesh.

Who is he kidding? Getting inked doesn't turn him on—it's an excuse, nothing more. It's Chris that gets his blood pumping, his heart hammering, his dick stiff. It's always been Chris.

He wears his tightest jeans, not so much for looks but because they constrict around an erection like a gloved hand. He has a cock ring on under them, too, and no underwear to add to the sensation. His balls hang low—if Chris pokes at them tonight, Lee's sure to feel it. He's been waiting *years* for that touch. He won't miss it a second time.

A clean white tank top completes the look. It's August in Richmond, hot and sticky out, and he likes showing off the ink on his arms. Chris's handiwork is drawn onto every inch of his skin, and Lee's damn proud to let others know he's a marked man. With a last look in the mirror and a wet comb run through his hair in some attempt to tame it, he heads out the door at a quick trot, hoping he doesn't hit any of the lights between his place and Tattoo 804. Even if he's late, though, he knows Chris will wait for him. They have a date...though Lee doesn't let himself think of it like that.

*A date.* The word implies so much more than what they have together. So much more Lee would like.

Outside the tattoo parlor, he pulls to a stop at the curb and is surprised to see Chris already outside. Hands shoved into the pockets of his own painted-on jeans, Chris leans against the bus stop sign in front of the building. His eyes look hooded and mysterious in the dying sunlight, and his hair is tousled from running his hand through it to keep it from his face. Lee's heart skips a beat—though Chris isn't exactly a Hollywood hottie, something about him always seems to take Lee's breath away. Lee should tell him sometime, he knows, but there's that other guy in the picture at the moment. Once he's gone, though...

*Who am I kidding?* Lee leans across the passenger side to roll down the window as Chris saunters over to his car. *I've had all the time in the world to tell him and I ain't said shit yet. Why ruin what we have now?* How'd they ever get back this easy camaraderie between them if Chris didn't feel the same way Lee does? *That's* what's stopping him from saying anything. He'd rather have any little piece of his friend he could than nothing at all.

Chris leans into the window once it's down. "Hey," he says with a grin. "Change of plans. You feel like clubbing a bit?"

At first Lee thinks he's joking. "What?"

Chris reaches in and unlocks the passenger side door. Before he drops into the seat beside Lee, he unlocks the door behind him as well. "April's got free passes into Toad's and wants us to tag along. Barry's band is playing there tonight—can you believe it? Toad's! That's like a major gig for them."

Barry, yes, of course. That explains the glint in Chris's eye and the excitement in his voice. Lee's smile feels tight across his face as he puts the car into neutral. "Toad's. Cool. We going?"

"You have to meet him," Chris is saying. He glances back at the parlor but the doors are shut, the lights inside out. Leaning across Lee, he hits the horn on the steering wheel with a short blast. "C'mon, April. Hurry the hell up."

As if the horn triggered a reaction, the door to the tattoo parlor opens and two, three, *four* giggling women tumble out. "Christ," Lee mutters under his breath.

They're all in their twenties, scantily clad, with high heels and teased hair. There's more ink on their legs, arms, and midriffs than clothing. Three of the girls huddle together while a fourth—April, Lee recognizes her from the parlor's reception desk—locks the door behind them. She tugs on it once to ensure it's latched, then leads her friends to Lee's car. They tumble into the back seat like Keystone Kops. The stench of sharp perfume hits Lee at once, and the sound of breathy giggles drowns out the song on his stereo. Mini-skirts are pulled down, tight T-shirts readjusted, as the four of them squeeze together. Lee glances into the rear-view mirror and just sees a row of painted faces smiling back.

It's going to be a *long* night.

He knows April by sight—she's part Asian, so she stands out from her friends. The other three sort of all look the same, white, perky, cute. Two are blonde and the third looks like she tried dying dark hair the same bleached shade and got a head full of honey-colored curls instead of pure white strands. Every time Lee looks back at them, that one with the honey hair is staring back. When their eyes meet in the rear-view mirror, she gives him a saucy wink he chooses to ignore. Just like he's ignoring the hand Chris rests on the space between the front seats, a hand that taps out a beat from the radio and nudges Lee's hip with every other note.

*We aren't alone*, Lee reminds himself. *Christ, we're going to see his boyfriend play.* But that does little to stem the start of an erection filling the front of his jeans.

Toad's is downtown near the Canal Walk, in a section of the city so low in altitude it's called the Bottom. Lee knows in theory where it is, but he's never been, so the first time he drives down the cobbled street where he thinks it's located, he turns before he reaches the water and misses the club completely. A harried drive around one-way streets through Shockhoe Bottom and he gets back to where he needs to be only to find there's no parking nearby. Oh, there's a deck, but, God damn it—he refuses to pay seven bucks to park in the same city where he lives. His mood darkens as he begins to crawl through the side streets, looking for somewhere to stop…

He's just about to head back to Toad's and drop off the giggling girls at the club just to get rid of them and let himself *think* when that hand Chris keeps between them touches Lee's thigh. "There," he says, pointing at an empty spot at the end of the block that isn't flanked by No Parking signs.

At first Lee doesn't respond. He can't—his mind is whirling out in a blur from that casual hand still resting high up on his thigh. *Little to the left,* he prays, holding his breath. *A few inches that way and you'll know it isn't your tattoo skills that turn me on.*

Chris gives his leg a squeeze. *Damn.* "Lee? Right there. We can walk."

With a glance over his shoulder that shows him nothing of the road—just a quartet of girlish smiles and batting lashes— Lee cuts across two lanes to pull into the spot. His hand brushes Chris's when he pulls up the parking brake, and he yanks on the brake a bit harder than necessary. "We're here."

The girls tumble out in a rush, then stand on the street corner like half-priced hookers running a two-for-one special. In the car's bright interior light, Chris flashes Lee a quick grin, then climbs out after his friends. There is one brief moment where Lee considers putting the car back into gear and tearing away from the curb—just leaving Chris and the girls to fend for themselves and heading back home. An evening alone *has* to be better than watching Chris drool over his new boy toy, right?

Right?

But Lee can't do that, not to Chris. So he unbuckles his belt and pulls the key from the ignition, resigned. At least Toad's has a full bar. Enough booze in his system and Lee won't give a fuck who Chris flirts with tonight.

Chris leads the way, practically racing through the back alleys and side streets to reach the club. The girls teeter on high heels as they hurry to keep up, and Lee trails behind, reluctant but unable to do anything but follow. He watches his steel-toed boots move over the cobbled street, his mind blank, his face devoid of emotion. When someone ahead of him stumbles, he almost runs her over without noticing.

She catches his arm as he passes, her red-tipped nails digging into his skin like claws. It's the honey blonde, and this close Lee notices how dried out and frizzy the dye has made her hair. With a winning smile, she leans against him as she wobbles unsteadily on her heels. "Hi there," she purrs, looking up with half-closed eyes. "My name's Melanie."

Lee tries to shake her off and can't. "Hey."

The others are drawing ahead. Lee starts after them and finds this Melanie chick holding him back. "You're Lee, right?" If she knows already, why's she bother to ask? With a throaty giggle, she whispers, "Chris says you're gay."

Lee plucks her fingers off his arm one by one. "Chris is right."

If he hopes that will deter her, he's mistaken. "I love gay boys," she gushes, launching herself at him before he can move out of reach. As she lays against his back, he feels pert little breasts push into his shoulder. "I think it's hot when two guys go at it, you know? *So* hot."

Lee drops all pretense and shoves her away. "Back up, bitch," he growls.

Before she can respond, he storms after Chris, who has stopped at the corner and waits, hands on his hips, for everyone to catch up. Lee glares at his friend as he approaches, but the grin on Chris's face only widens. "What?"

Without answering, Lee keeps walking. Chris falls into step beside him and drapes an arm around Lee's shoulder. "This is great," he says, excitement evident in his voice. Lee's glad one of them feels that way. "I'm so happy you finally get to meet Barry. You'll love him, I just know it."

Lee has his doubts.

DESPITE THE EARLY hour, Toad's is hopping. Chris leads his friends around to the canal entrance, where April hands their passes to a bouncer blocking twin glass doors that vibrate from the pounding music inside. Once they're waved through, Chris takes the stairs two at a time to reach the second floor, then hurries down the bare corridor to the open door of the club. Inside, the lights are doused, pitching the club into darkness; the only illumination comes from the stage, where Barry's band is already playing. Chris pushes through the mass of bumping bodies, grinding between strangers as he shoves toward the stage. He manages to get up close—this is a small club, and there's nothing separating the stage from the dance floor, so Chris bullies his way into the crowd until he's right up front. Barry's on bass guitar above Chris, eyes shut, fingers ripping over his strings, completely lost in the music. Chris calls his name like a rabid fan, then whoops loudly, but the guitar riff drowns him out. Still, he raises his arms in the air and sways in time to the beat, letting the people around him move his body as the music washes over him. That's his man.

Some time later, Barry sees him and winks. Happy his boyfriend knows he's here, Chris drifts back to the bar, where he finds Lee glaring at the trio of giggling girls who fawn around him. April is nowhere to be seen, but her friends sigh over Lee as he guzzles down a beer straight from the bottle. Sidling up behind his friend, Chris claps Lee on the back and shouts to be heard over the noise. "How many have you had so far?"

"I lost count," Lee hollers back.

With a laugh, Chris signals the bartender and orders what Lee's drinking. He takes the seat between his friend and the girls, then points at the stage. "I'm dating the guy on guitar."

The girl who hit on Lee earlier shrieks. "Oh, my God! That's *so* hot!"

Chris thinks so, too. But when he turns to grin at Lee, he sees something troubling in his friend's expression, a haunted look in Lee's eyes that disappears before he can comment on it. Leaning closer, Chris asks, "You okay, man?"

Lee tips his bottle as if he's toasting Chris. "I'm cool. So that's him?"

A goofy grin threatens to split Chris's face. "Yeah. God, he's fine. And in bed? Shit. Don't get me started."

Lee doesn't. He eyes the stage warily, his face an unreadable mask as he drinks down the last of his beer, but when he sets the bottle on the bar, he smiles at Chris and that seems to chase away the shadows haunting his features. "That good, huh?"

"Dude…" Chris drawls, nodding his head.

Suddenly April appears between them, elbowing her way to the bar. As she waves her bottle of beer at the bartender, she glances at Lee and notices the new tattoo Chris inked onto his shoulder. "Sweet!" She pulls the strap on Lee's tank top aside to get a better look. "This is wild, man. How long did it take?"

If there's anything Chris likes to talk about more than his boyfriend, it's his tattoos. Sliding off his stool, he steps around April to tug up the bottom of Lee's shirt. "You have to see the full thing to appreciate it. Isn't it awesome?"

April's friends circle around for a look. Lee slumps his shoulders and hunches over the bar, a low growl in the back of his throat. "Chris, really…"

"Let them look," Chris chides. He runs a hand down Lee's bare back—the skin is warm beneath his palm, familiar. He intimately knows the curve of Lee's spine, the freckles that dot his flesh, the three moles right below his ribs that form Orion's Belt—the constellation was one of Chris's first tattoos. The girls ooh over the dragon bones that trail down the center of Lee's back; they love the intricate piping Chris finished last week, the colors still bright. Proud of his work, Chris beams as they comment on the tattoos, their polished nails tracing the lines of ink.

After a few moments, Lee shrugs them away. "All right, already. Get off me, will you?"

"Just showing off my portfolio," Chris teases.

As he starts to smooth down Lee's shirt, one of the girls notices something just above the waistband of Lee's jeans. "What's this?"

Chris glimpses the tip of a tiger's tail and laughs. "That's one of my best. Lee's year of the tiger, see, in Chinese astrology?" The girls nod, but from their vacant expressions, he knows they don't have a clue what he's talking about. Still, it's one of his best tattoos to date. Tugging down a little on Lee's pants, Chris points to the orange and black swirl that comprises the tail of his abstract, Asian-inspired tiger. The beast runs from Lee's waist down to his upper thigh. "This one's bitchin'. You can't see it all but Lee, pop your fly. Let's give the girls a show."

He tugs again on Lee's jeans as the girls giggle, and is surprised when he hears his friend tell him, "No."

The word sounds so foreign in Lee's voice that Chris refuses to believe he said it. "Show off a bit," Chris says, spinning Lee around on the bar stool. As his friend chugs back another beer, Chris fumbles with the button on the front of Lee's jeans. "Come on, they ain't going to see anything major. I just want to show them the tiger—"

"No." Lee's hand drops to his lap and pushes Chris away. "Not here."

Too late. Chris has the fly undone and starts to unzip Lee's jeans. "So they see your undies," he chides, laughing. "So what? Unless you're not wearing any…"

That thought tapers off as the zipper eases down inch by

inch and Chris sees no fabric beneath it. No jock strap, no tighty whities, no boxers. Lee isn't looking at him—his hard gaze is off in the distance somewhere, a million miles away from this crowded bar and the girls huddled around behind Chris. When the first curly strands of dark hair peek through Lee's open fly, Chris covers them with his hand to hide them from view. His laugh now sounds forced. "Christ, Lee. Why didn't you tell me you were free-balling?"

Now his friend's gaze shifts to find Chris. The expression in those bright blue eyes is unreadable. "What's it to you what underwear I'm wearing?"

"Or *not* wearing." Chris tries to rezip the jeans, but the tiny metal teeth catch in Lee's skin, leaving red little bite marks behind. An awkwardness descends over Chris—this isn't happening, it can't be, and why the hell isn't Lee helping him out here? He pokes under the zipper, ignoring the flutter of soft skin and the faint curls that tickle his fingertips as he tries to undo the damage he's done. Lee's staring off again, past Chris's shoulder, at something only he can see. With a growl, Chris mutters, "Lee, damn it. Help a man out here, will you?"

Suddenly from behind him comes Barry's voice, a hard edge to it. "What the hell is this?"

Chris turns, hands still shoved into Lee's pants, and sees his boyfriend glaring at the two of them. In the overhead lights from the bar his disheveled hair looks greasy and unkempt, his face shiny with sweat, but it's his eyes that catch Chris's attention, his *eyes* that won't let Chris look away. They burn with a singular intensity, brows knit together above them, a mix of distrust and confirmation blazing in their depths.

"Barry," Chris sighs. He tugs on the zipper one last time and catches a knuckle in its teeth for his effort. Then Lee's hands brush his away, *finally*, and Chris turns to grin at his boyfriend. "God, you guys rocked up there. This is—"

"I know who he is." Barry's words are short, each clipped in anger Chris doesn't yet understand. "What I *don't* know is why you had your hands down the front of his damn *pants.*"

"I wasn't…" Chris turns to Lee in mute appeal, but Lee's impassive gaze is trained on Barry and he doesn't see Chris's silent plea for help. "I was showing the girls his tattoo, Barry. Honest, that's all it was. He has this really great tiger I did—"

"Where? On his dick?"

Chris tries to laugh that off but Barry turns on his heel and shoves through the crowd, away from them. "Jeez," Chris mutters, then raises his voice over the noise to holler, "Barry! Wait!"

He doesn't.

Before he can disappear Chris heads after him, leaving Lee behind with the girls. He pushes strangers aside, catching elbows in his side and ducking under arms stretched out as if to stop him. Ahead, Barry hits the exit door with one hard fist and ducks out into the brightly lit hall beyond. Chris is only a few steps behind him; the door doesn't manage to latch before Chris rams through it. Barry's ahead, and with no crowd to impede him, Chris races to catch up. "Barry, please. Stop."

When his hand falls on Barry's shoulder, his boyfriend shrugs it off. He turns, his face lit with torment, his eyes wet with unshed tears. "What the *fuck* do you want, Chris?"

"Barry…" Chris catches his breath and tries to take Barry's hand in his. He holds tight to Barry's little finger as if grasping for straws. "It's not what you think. I was only—"

"No." Barry closes his hand into a fist, squeezing Chris's fingers painfully. "It's not what *you* think. I knew it all along."

Exasperated, Chris asks, "Knew *what*? He's my friend, Barry. I've known him since the fourth grade! There's nothing between us. Believe me, I've never screwed around with him, *never.* And sure as hell not since I've been with you. I'm not that kind of guy."

With his free hand, Barry wipes under his eye, careful not to smudge his make-up. He sighs, a defeated sound, and seems to deflate a little before Chris. Despite the venue and the few people passing by, despite the crowd inside the bar and Barry's band mates wandering somewhere nearby, Chris wants nothing more than to take Barry in his arms, hold him close, and take away the doubt and pain twisting on his face. But when he moves closer, Barry's words stop him in his tracks. "I know you're not. But you're half in love with him and I can't stand it."

Chris laughs, relieved. That's ridiculous. "Barry, jeez. I am *not*—"

"You *are*." Barry rubs his hand across his nose as he sniffles. "Don't deny it, babe. Hell, you may not even *know* it, but you are. He's all you talk about twenty-four seven. Whenever we're together it's Lee this and Lee that. It's like living in a threesome without getting laid by both guys. I've always shared you with him, *always*."

"Barry—"

But Barry shakes his head and pulls his fingers free from Chris's hand. "Believe me, Chris. I've dealt with it long enough and I can't take it any more. I just can't. The only time you talk about your work is to tell me what new tattoos you've given Lee. He's first on the speed dial on your cell. I know—I looked. Most of your calls are to him, not me. You spend hours together after everyone else has left the parlor and he's inked in places I don't want to think of you seeing, let alone *touching*, and…" Another sigh, this one so sad, it breaks Chris's heart to hear it. "And he likes you back. Don't say he doesn't."

Chris forces a laugh that sounds fake to his own ears. "Barry, really. You've got it all wrong—"

"Do I?" Barry stares at Chris, his face hardened now, his emotions masked. "Did you even notice the look on his face when you were touching his crotch? Or have you seen it so often before, you don't realize what you're seeing anymore?"

The NEXT TIME Chris calls, Lee hesitates before he agrees to anything. "This isn't another scheme to get me to go clubbing with you guys, is it?" he asks, dubious, when Chris wants him to swing by the parlor after closing. "Because, dude, you ditched me and I had to fend off three very drunk-ass girls the rest of the night."

"Naw, man." Chris laughs, a warm sound through the tinny receiver on Lee's cell. "I got a new design I want to draw and you're my canvas. My *muse*, even. You coming?"

*Keep talking like that and I will*, Lee thinks, but he keeps that to himself. Instead he grunts into the phone, noncommittal, but Chris knows him so well, he just laughs again. "See you at eight."

Lee is sure to wear a pair of boxer briefs under his faded Levis *this* time. He arrives at quarter to, like usual. The place looks empty—April's not behind the counter like she normally is and Chris's booth is hidden behind a black folding screen. The buzz of a tattoo needle can be heard over the rush of air from the AC. Knocking on the counter as he steps around it, Lee calls out, "Yo, Chris?"

The buzzing stops. "Back here."

As Lee approaches the screen, he hears a woman ask, "That your friend? The gay one?"

"God," Lee mutters. "Tell everyone, will you?"

Chris laughs as the needles flare to life again. "Come on around, Lee. Check this out."

On the other side of the screen, a woman lies on her back in Chris's tattooing chair. She's topless, her long blonde hair in dreads and secured into a ponytail on top of her head. She has piercings in her nose and both eyebrows and lays beneath Chris's needle, her small hands holding aside her breasts as Chris inks a large purple and pink butterfly onto the center of her chest. From the smears of ink and faint traces of blood that discolor her pale skin, Lee knows they've been here a while. Chris is on the very last bit of the left wing, filling in a curlicue that curves over her ribs.

When she sees Lee, she grins. Her lipstick is black, making her look ghastly. "What do you think?"

Lee whistles low. "Man, that's wicked. How long's it taken?"

Chris shrugs as he finishes up. "Couple hours. You like?"

"You're amazing," Lee tells him. He doesn't mean just the design or the tight colors, either, but Chris doesn't have to know that.

It takes another ten minutes before the customer is pulling on an oversized T-shirt, the cellophane covering her fresh tattoo crackling as she dresses. Lee waits, hands in his pockets, as she tips Chris and he lets her out the front door. Once it's locked behind her, he steps over to where Lee is, leafing through a book of pre-fabricated tattoo designs. Without warning, Chris leans heavily against Lee's back, his weight warm and welcome and so damn unexpected, Lee's dick hardens in his jeans. "You ready for me?" Chris wants to know.

His breath tickles Lee's ear and, for one precious moment, neither move. Lee wants to reach behind him, touch Chris's waist, keep him close, but he's afraid any move he makes will ruin things between them. So he waits until Chris steps back and tugs on one of Lee's belt loops. "Come on, Lee. Your turn."

Lee forces a grin as he follows Chris. "I sure hope you're not planning on putting a butterfly smack in the middle of my chest," he says, trying to lighten the mood between them. Why does he feel awkward all of a sudden? He's been alone with Chris before. Hiding his true feelings for his friend has become second nature to him now. "Maybe something cool, like a torn wound with a beating heart exposed, or ribs, or something that's not quite so girly, you know?"

With a laugh, Chris disappears behind the screen. Lee follows, but before he can take a seat in Chris's chair, his friend shakes his head. "Jeans come off. No chest tat for you today. I'm going lower."

Fear seizes Lee's heart. God, with the hard-on he's sporting? Oh, *hell* no. Grasping at his belt buckle, Lee starts, "Chris, I don't think—"

"Come on," Chris cajoles. "Don't get all shy on me now.

Unless you're going commando again?"

"No, I've got on skivvies. But—"

Chris shakes his head. "No buts. Take it off, sexy. Let me see what we're working with here."

Lee's heart beats in his throat as he unbuckles his belt. When he unbuttons his jeans, his zipper eases down on its own beneath his erection. He fists the front of his boxer briefs, hoping to hide the bulge there, but Chris is busy getting his inks ready and isn't paying Lee any attention. Quickly Lee strips out of the jeans and hops into the chair, pulling at his crotch to make the material look like it's just puckering up on its own. As Chris unpacks a fresh needle, Lee jokes, "I wonder what your boyfriend would think if he saw us like this. What's his name again?"

"Barry," Chris answers. His voice sounds a little off somehow, not quite as bright as it was before. "And he's not my boyfriend any more."

Part of Lee wants to whoop with delight, but he manages to contain himself. He hopes he sounds sincere when he says, "That sucks. What happened?"

Chris shrugs. "We broke up."

"Well, duh." Lee shifts in the chair, raising the knee closest to Chris in an effort to hide his crotch from his friend. His dick has a mind of its own, it seems; once it heard Barry was out of the picture, it stood up at attention and wanted in the conversation. Lee wonders if he can excuse himself for a few hot moments in the bathroom alone to show it who's boss. "When did this go down?"

"At Toad's." Chris still isn't looking at him, which gives Lee an excuse to study his friend. Though there's a lingering sadness about his mouth and eyes, Chris doesn't seem overly upset about losing a guy he once called *the one*. "That night we went, remember? We got into it after he found us with my hands down your pants."

Lee snickers. He remembers *that* all too well—those few moments still give him enough to fantasize about when he jerks off. "Dude, we weren't even...I mean, you told him, right? It was completely innocent. Shit, you barely even saw my pubes."

A faint smile crosses Chris's face. "He knew that. But we got to talking and he said some things I hadn't even thought about before, things that really got me thinking, you know?"

"What kinds of things?" Lee asks. He thinks he knows. From the sinking feeling in the pit of his stomach, he isn't sure he wants to hear Chris repeat them.

Chris takes a moment to strip off the latex gloves he's wearing. They're tossed into the trash, and a fresh pair is plucked from the box on Chris's desk. He sets them next to the little cups of ink he has arranged there. Then he wheels his stool over to where Lee sits. Guiding Lee's knees apart, Chris glides in between them, hands on Lee's ankles. The sadness is gone from his face now. A fierce glow has replaced it, igniting the depths of Chris's eyes until Lee can't tear his gaze away from his friend. The hands on Lee's ankles start to rub up his calves, pushing down his socks to smooth over hairy skin. "Things about you," Chris says softly. Lee covers his crotch with both hands to hide it from view. "Things about us I never noticed before."

Lee's voice sounds like it comes from a million miles away when he murmurs, "There is no us. We're just friends."

That faint smile is back, ghosting over Chris's mouth, curving his lips. Lee stares at it so long, he doesn't realize it's coming closer until he hears the squeal of Chris's stool when it pushes out from under him. Then Chris is leaning above him, the hands on Lee's legs ruffling his hair as they smooth up to his knees, then over his thighs. They're in his lap, Chris's hands, covering Lee's own for a moment before easing beneath Lee's fingers to brush over the front of Lee's boxer briefs. His dick jerks beneath Chris's touch, dampening the fabric that separates them. Chris's breath fans over Lee's upper lip and those eyes stare into his own, larger than life and closer than Lee ever imagined them to be.

When Chris speaks, his words are mere breath against Lee's

mouth. "We don't have to settle for just that," he purred. "If you're interested in something more…"

Lee always has been. He kisses away the rest of Chris's words, every fiber of his being crying out in triumph. *Yes.*

# *About the Author*

J.M. SNYDER LIVES in Richmond, Virginia. A graduate of George Mason University, Snyder is a multi-published, best-selling author of gay erotic and romantic fiction who has worked with several e-publishers, most notably Amber Allure Press, eXcessica, and Torquere Press. Snyder's short stories have appeared online and in anthologies by Alyson Books, Cleis Press, and others.

In 2010, Snyder started JMS Books LLC to publish and promote her own writing as well as queer fiction, nonfiction, and poetry she enjoys.

Positive feedback as well as hate mail can be forwarded to the author at jms@jmsnyder.net.

Made in the USA
Coppell, TX
25 May 2022